FIC   Hawkins, Bobbie
       Louise, 1930-

       One small saga

One Small Saga

BOBBIE LOUISE HAWKINS :: A NOVELLA

Coffee House Press :: Saint Paul, Minnesota

The publishers wish to thank the National Endowment for the Arts, a federal agency, for a Small Press Assistance Grant that aided in the production of this book.

Fic

Designed by Allan Kornblum. Calligraphy by Glenn Epstein. Composition by Annie Graham, Iowa City, Iowa.

R0042736825

Coffee House Press books are distributed by:
Bookslinger
213 East Fourth Street
St. Paul, MN 55101

Library of Congress Cataloging in Publication Data

Hawkins, Bobbie Louise, 1930–
    One small saga.

    I. Title.
PS 3553.R3405   1984   813'.54   84–15612
ISBN 0–918273–05–6

ONE SMALL SAGA

The Bride

In late November on a warm afternoon with no breeze
in it a man and a woman sat high up a gravelly slope
overlooking the thin thread of water still called the Rio
Grande.
We had shed our sweaters into a small pile on either
side, his and hers.
There's that intimacy in even the slightest stripping, Oh,
do let me help you with your wraps, my dear, and why
not forever while we're about it.
He had just proposed marriage again.
I was quiet but not as if I gave it serious consideration.
It would serve him right if I said yes.
What to consider as if the house were burning.
I looked sideways at this eligible suitor. Pale hair slightly
curling. Pale eyes. An immediately intimate smile. An
insistently cheerful disposition. Tenacity.
I wondered at it.
I seemed to myself such an unlikely candidate for so
Jane Austen an advantage.

KING KONG had played in a movie house in Lagos in Nigeria for twelve years. For a few cents apiece, Axel said, Africans who came to town out of the bush had made it a weekly ritual.

The print of the film was old and scratched. The giant ape appeared from and disappeared into mists of light, a radiant fabric, a magic shining of scratched film.

The movie house, a warehouse room, would be filled with African blacks watching Hollywood blacks say "Magumba!" and "Kumbawa!"

They watched a Hollywood ape with mad glass eyes crash free, destroy the El, climb the Empire State Building.

When the time came for the ape to be shot down the room would be very quiet.

And he would fall.

In Denmark no one would think to marry a virgin. (This was 1950.)

So that was that; no problem that only yesterday would have been an admission. Not really shameful, more usual than acknowledged. But now it seemed it was a bonus.

"Who wants all that mess," he asked.

"I don't," he answered.

He had been first a blond head poked around the screen put just inside the studio door to keep passersby from looking in at the nude models. (Window washers had a field day.) He was a blond head and an English accent asking whether there was an office for the Art Department and where it might be.

I was standing wiping paint off a fistful of brushes with newspaper.

I stopped, my hands filled, gave him directions.

He bobbed thanks and disappeared.

"There's no one there. Do you think they've gone for
lunch?"
"They should be back by one-thirty."
He was in full figure and smiling.
I'd thrown the wads of newspaper into the bin and was
swishing the bristles in turpentine.
What were colors had melted to mud on my hands.
"I haven't had lunch," he said. "Would you like to go to
lunch?"

The brushes were washed, rinsed, wiped damp dry, put
stems down in a mason jar where the cleaned heads
fanned out in a damp bouquet.
It was already an age-old story.

He took me to lunch. Took me to dinner. Took me to
lunch the next day and showed me chess moves.
And proposed marriage.
He didn't want to return to Denmark and remarry his
first wife who was making overtures. He didn't tell me
that.

He said I should leave this place. I agreed and would
have been gone long ago but didn't know how.
Even with all he implied, I told him No.
I wanted over the falls in a mindless rush. Love is when
you can't help yourself.
He said that could all come later.
"It would be different if there were more time," he said.

The Rio Grande has shrunk with age and demand. Its
banks hold, spread wide in a fixed memory of better
days.
Now it is mostly sand with stands of tamarisk and cot-
tonwood along the edges.

The cottonwoods were filled with dried brown leaves, all their fiery gold faded.

He hadn't seen that. At least I knew more about this place where we were than he did.

He had no idea that his worldly knowledge, which he meant to be tempting, Europe and London and Africa, also caused me to look askance.

I was not so charmed as he was by the sense of myself as young and precocious and malleable. I was not so charmed that he saw me as improvable and himself as my transforming agent.

When I implied I liked myself well enough he would smile and know better.

It was all very unsatisfying for him.

This young woman did not know that in his own environment, in Lagos, where he was chief architect and manager of his English firm's West African branch, he was a more than usually desirable bachelor. Mothers invited him to dinner as a hope for their unmarried daughters.

He had never thought to marry an American.

His friends had said, "Don't come back with an American wife," and it had been a joke. It took no thought at all.

His sense of American women was of females with their hair frozen in place, dressed in pastel nylon. Voices located in nasal passages.

"You don't sound like an American," he said, and meant it to be a compliment.

He watched her look down the valley and not say Yes and he wondered whether it might simply be that she was ignorant of true values.

If she agreed to marry him and they left this place would she, once they were beyond those mountains, change? Would she know what mattered? And knowing it would she respond appropriately?
If not, what a burden it would be to have a wife who might, through youthful ignorance, go vague in the very face of worth.

"If you marry him would your children be American or Danish?"
"Oh, I don't know. You can probably choose."
"Well, you'd make them be American, wouldn't you?"
My mother stood in the sunshine holding a willow-pattern cup in her left hand, a square of unbleached muslin in her right.

He tempted me deliberately.
He said, "If you don't want to stay you can come back. We can always get a divorce. A divorce isn't so much."
He said, "If you'd rather, we can have a trial marriage for a year and see at the end of it whether we want to marry."
He even suggested to my mother that we could have a trial marriage.
He suggested the trial marriage to my mother as a way to reassure her. My mother was not reassured.
But I was impressed that he did it.
It amazed me that he did it.
I was impressed enough to say Yes on the strength of it.

In Florida they were teaching porpoises to talk.
The announcer said that in captivity the porpoises lower their voice pitch toward the range of their human captors.
"If that isn't the silliest thing!" my mother said.
"What would *you* do," the announcer asked, "if an in-

telligent life form had you caught in an air-filled case and you must try to communicate with them?"

"I think I'll go with Axel," I said into the room.

If someone had made a joke of it I might still have been stopped.

"Well, if that's the way you want it, honey."

And he?

He twisted slightly.

Had he been enjoying an increasing security in my refusals?

"Well?" I asked when we stepped outside into the night.

My eyes felt altered by decision. Was it a decision?

"I wish you had said something to me first. It's all right to surprise your mother but you might have found a more private time to tell me."

I knew he was right but thought he really wanted us to act as if we were in love.

And why not.

In love or not it was a romance.

The desires of the heart do rise up at the least jogging. The heart stands high and looks for miles at the least excuse.

The engagement was effected.

We regarded one another, intent. The night sky darkened. We were in each other's life. The moon was a definite and vivid crescent. Very thin. Very thin. The ancient horns.

On the morning of the wedding day a snapshot was taken of the couple. They are standing in the backyard of a small square house. Some clothes have been washed and are hanging on a line to the right. The groom-to-be is wearing crepe-soled shoes and a belted jacket. The bride-to-be is wearing Levi pants and a man's white

shirt. A bandanna is tied around her head to hide the
curlers. She means to be beautiful later.

It was a grander solution, that marriage, than any I
could have dreamed of prior to the arrival of Axel in his
belted jacket. I was at the end of my rope and the rope
itself had been an invention.

I had borrowed money from a loan company to pay the
first half of a semester's tuition (Fine Arts Department,
University of New Mexico, Albuquerque). My plan
was to find a job that would both leave me free during
the day so I could go to class and pay me enough money
to let me repay the loan while I saved toward the second
half of the tuition.

I found no job that fit the projection.

When Axel appeared in the doorway I was dead broke
and stopped. I had no money for the loan's current payment and I had no money for the balance of the tuition.

In painting class I had come to be more experimental
daily as I used up tubes of color and made do with what
was left.

My drawing teacher thought I showed up at class after
class with only a newsprint pad and charcoal because I
couldn't be bothered to bring whatever he had assigned
as that day's media. He told me that earlier he had
thought of me as someone with promise, someone special, and I was a disappointment.

I knew that I could explain to him so he would know I
was not shirking. And I knew that if I tried to explain I
would begin crying. I was not insensitive.

I did not try to explain.

All my hopes for self-improvement had brought me to
no next move, no resource for one more step.

And in my more intimate daily life I was not only not a virgin but I had been brainwashed to believe I would pay for that failing, and to feel (I can't call it thinking) that without a great deal of luck and perseverance (in what I don't remember) I could only go downhill.
At nineteen I was blighted and stopped.
And then. . . .

I was married, all unknowing, by an FBI agent.
He was the minister for the St. John's African Holiness Church.
I was a member of the NAACP and so was he.
When I needed a preacher he was the only preacher I knew.
People more sophisticated and knowledgeable than I was and am have been taken in by FBI agents in whatever drag their cover story required.

I learned the truth of it when I returned to Albuquerque six years later.
Of course I've always assumed he really *was* a preacher and we really *were* married.

• • •

It took just two weeks from the day they met for the handsome Dane to marry his young wife and put the two of them aboard a Greyhound Bus, enroute to Africa.
They would stop to see his sister, Birte.
They would stop in New York City.
They would stop in Denmark.
They would stop in London.
Then they would take the last leg "home".

Birte told Axel of the cheap passage she had found to

Denmark.
An old Swedish liner, the *Gripsholm*, reclaimed from the
bone-yard to be a hospital ship during the war, was now
a passenger ship for travelers with no grand expecta-
tions.
Birte would be on it with her two children in ten days.
After Christmas in Denmark she would go to her own
house in London and be joined there by her excellent
husband, Gilbert, in mid-January.
Gilbert, who never spoke when Birte was talking, stood
at the piano picking out calypsos with one finger.
Axel telephoned.
In ten days Axel and I would also be aboard the *Gripsholm*.

Axel did not think of himself as capricious.
When he was younger he had, for a bet and a dare,
stripped naked and jumped off the railing of a Swedish
freighter in a pitch black night to fall far down into the
unknown waters of a Russian harbor where they were
moored. His instantly sobered companions had called a
deckhand and he had been got back aboard without
much trouble.
He enjoyed heroic status for the rest of that voyage.

"You are *insane*, my dear Axel! You are quite *insane!*"
Birte laughed as she spoke. She cut her own hair and the
thick-cropped shelf showed her thick neck. She spoke
vigorously and laughed. Her eyes were blue and critical,
taking inventory. When she laughed she exposed large
strong teeth. When she walked the floor shook.
"You are such *romantics!*" she said to me, meaning
nothing admirable.
Birte had survived the Battle of Britain. Birte had hated
the American soldiers who arrived in London saying
"Remember Pearl Harbor."

"They married the worst women imaginable. I must say we cheered them on. It looked for a time as if the Americans might be the solution to cleaning up Picadilly. All the whores went to America as war-brides." She smiled at me.

I said Yes and meant it.
I meant to be a wife however confused I might be by the terms.
In my heart of hearts I had made promises to the future.
I would do my best to not botch it.
I meant to do it right.
I meant all sorts of things Axel had no notion of.
I *would* get on with this beastly woman I was now related to.
I smiled at Birte.
It was very like smiling at a locomotive.

• • •

Hotel wallpaper.
Being caught in somebody else's idea.
Three thousand miles from what I knew best and farther still to go.
Back is no direction.

Axel clicked suitcases, opened and closed drawers.
Axel began to whistle while he worked.
Axel meant to jolly me up.

In the meantime he suffered his own misgivings.
He was, after all, no Pygmalion.
Hard marble and a chisel to work it with are a far cry from a lump of unmoving female and a cheerful whistle.
Still he whistled.
Hope can do no less.

I came out of bed glued to a tumble of covers. My feet reached the carpeted floor and I stood, looked at the wall for a count of ten, headed for the bathroom with the lurching unevenness of an adolescent.
Axel sighed a sigh of exasperation and relief. And when I came back out of the bathroom carrying the toothpaste and my toothbrush I smiled. Not vibrantly. Not courageously. But it was a smile.

New York City was ready for Christmas.
The taxi that took us to our ship drove past windows filled with seasonal displays. In one an animated Jack jumped over his candlestick and turned to jump again. And Peter Peter stood beside his pumpkin shell with its closed door and its window open to show Mrs. Peter within in a state of domestic felicity, her head nodding and nodding, a constant smile on her face.

America, Birte told me at dinner, did not have Bach or Beethoven or Karl Marx. America did not have Paris, the Greeks, or the Renaissance. America did not have Europe. And Birte, it seemed, did.

Birte spoke four languages, had a superior education, was married to a superior person. She came from a superior family from a superior country which did not preclude her being a holder of democratic views.

And I was not to take the taxi-driver from Chicago who shared our third-class table as representative of the type of person I would be associating with once we arrived in Denmark.

I said little in return.

Being overwhelmed by Birte was an acceptable response.

I did not envy the First Class passengers their carved Victorian bars, lounging rooms with flowers on writing tables.

I envied them for not having Birte.

Axel found a green marble swimming pool in the depths of the ship.

He found it by asking to look at the ship's plans.

And there it was, with its own little elevator up to all the levels of all the decks.

He went to where he had seen the elevator on the plans, pushed the button, went down. He came out of the elevator into a room the size of a high school gymnasium, fitted out like one. A bit more exotic. There were electric horses that could be set at three gaits. There were belts to trim the figure by shaking the body. There were barbells and dumbbells. And through a door at the room's far end was a smaller room just large enough to hold a full-size swimming pool with six feet around it to be walked on.

The pool was filled with blue-green water. A switch on the wall turned on lights at the pool bottom and made a light-show of wavering lines on the walls. The pool was green marble with curved steps at one end. Green marble pillars were every five feet along the other three sides. Each pillar held a brass ring and through the ring a thick wine-red velvet rope was threaded, making scallops around the pool.

Axel got permission to use the pool on the basis that he tell none of the other passengers about it.

We took towels daily and made our way along the iced deck to the elevator door. We spent our afternoons in the pool and the adjacent sauna.

I stopped sleeping.
It's the old songs we love the best... anxiety and floating phrases ... not all the time just chunks of it ...
I stopped sleeping.
I like high-class myself they get all that extra room for the generous moves ... and Hi-Yo, Silver ... Heigh-Ho as in Tote that barge?
I stopped sleeping.
Pills from the ship's doctor had a reverse effect given the dinner and the booze and the pigs' heads with items of fruit lodged between the opened lips on the corners of the tables and paper elves holding hands and dancing in long cut-out strips the length of the tables while the after-dinner speeches dealt with variations on Scandinavian-Scandinavian Brotherhood and Scandinavian-American Brotherhood and the Norwegians and Danes went tight-lipped at the Swedes saying so, the war being too close and Hitler using Sweden as a footpath to get to everywhere else.

Next day the Swedes left. All the barriers that designated the classes of passengers were taken down. The ship opened to be one big party all the way to the other two countries.

Two Danish reporters who came aboard in Sweden found Axel's name on the passenger list and sought him out to ask him whether he was related to his father.
Herr Politimester Raasloff commanded all the Danish police forces, an appointment from his friend, the King. When the Nazis had entered Denmark, Herr Raasloff had been one of the first persons to be put in a cell.
Axel explained to me that his father's position was nothing like being a policeman in the United States. His father's position was more prestigious and more honorable though it seemed it did not pay well. The honor was the thing.

NEWLYWEDS ON HONEYMOON was the story the reporters got, and pictures of the couple with confetti and streamers caught to their hair and shoulders.

During the interview Birte bristled, irritated by the lack of attention she was getting in all this.
She reminded them all that Axel was, in fact, her father's stepson while she is truly her father's daughter. One of the reporters mollified her with questions. She was satisfied until two days later when she saw the newspaper, with its headline and its large picture of her brother and his wife, and found that only the slightest mention had been made of her own presence.

• • •

This day of the small rain, the gray sky: this day was ours.
This landing place, flags flying, confetti caught to our

hair, tendrils of streamers caught to our coats.
On the dock a red-coated band was playing shining
brass.
The dock below was filled with upturned faces.
The *Gripsholm* had risen into the sky and these were our
own dear heliotropes.
Axel and Birte scanned the crowd for familar faces.
"There they are! They're waving!"
Birte snatched her daughter Squiggles high to wave to
Grand-Mama and Grand-Papa.
Squiggles had been told of the rail and doom, and
shrieked at being swung so easily into jeopardy.
She was put down and clung sobbing to the skirts of her
own Mommy-monster.
Birte's son, Charles, stood stalwartly watching, ap-
parently unmoved, very English, very masculine, very
much the nine-year-old young man who could take it all
in stride.

We came to earth in the drafty, echoing Customs building.

Change the country. Change the name.
"Girl of my dreams" . . . Set to start again and do it better
this time.
I held onto Axel's arm. I smiled wanly, pale and not at
my best.
I am a crumpled version and defenseless.

We all stood under a giant "R", though soon Birte would
go to stand under "M".
"My father could have exempted all our bags from in-
spection but he would never do such a thing," she told
me, and smiled in triumph at being like everyone else
but by a moral choice.

She also told me, "This will be a very good Christmas for you. We do not use electric lights on the tree."
"When my dream boat comes home," sang in my head, Birte won't be on it.

We went to the home of an Aunt who lived in Copenhagen. Tante Anna had married a Frenchman. He had lived in Denmark now for thirty years and still spoke only French. His wife cheerfully translated for him even though it was clear he understood all that was said.
After dinner I slipped away to a front room to look at Copenhagen through the parlor window's lace curtains. They found me there, sleeping, sitting in a small chair with my elbows on the window sill, my chin resting in my hands.
Fru Raasloff led me through the house to a small cold bedroom and tucked me under a goosedown cover.
Axel stood in the doorway explaining at length to his sister Gena, who was as thin as Birte was fat.
"Well," she said to him, her voice sour, "you've got yourself a child-of-nature."

Jørn the beautiful boy, eight years old, his yellow hair
and eyebrows a line straight across his face, red-cheeked
and vigorous, tramps the coastline in all weather. He
stands, eyes blue as birds flown to the horizon to return
in their own good time. His boots are made of heavy
black rubber and mash their print into the sand in his
wake. He returns in the late winter afternoon back
along his tracks to his own garden's gate. Over his head
bare branches twine and mesh in a lacework canopy.
The last of the pearly twilight seeps coldly through, and
the garden, darkening at the corners, grows larger. The
sitting room window flickers with warm color through
the crooked fruit trees. A scraggy skeleton of lilac
scratches his coat as he passes to go through the kitchen
door.

The kitchen air is steamy and flavored. Armandine, her
face shiny, moves among the clutter of cutlery, crock-
ery, rag-ends of trimmed fat. She smiles at him and
wishes him good evening. A light sweat of steam covers
the boy's face as he supports himself, hand on the wet
wall, and fights his boots off. In the narrow pantry window at his side all the panes of glass have run stripes of
small rivers from the top to the bottom.

The house is in threefold celebration: Christmas is near;
the family is together; Axel has brought home a bride.
They are all in the sitting room. Their faces are lighted
by candles among pine boughs on the room's central
table. It is the fire that lights the walls around them and
shows the old-fashioned room more clearly with its pictures and heavy, comfortable furnishings. They turn to
welcome him in, their most recent seafarer. He circles
the room formally, shaking hands with each of them
and bobbing his head.

Fru Raasloff is the room's coquette: charming, demanding, her gestures youthful. Her daughters are her tragedy. Birte sits in a chair, large and heavy, with a jolly
maliciousness. Gena, thin and quince-mouthed, soon to
be divorced, sits on the curving love seat. They are the
traditional "two ugly sisters." They have never learned
to "enter" a room.

"Ah," Fru Raasloff will say in the next breath after such a
sad admission, "but my *sons* are delightful!"

Axel and Jørn were accustomed to their mother's un-
qualified approval.

Fru Raasloff is attempting English for her new daughter-
in-law.

She names something, adds a verb. It makes no sense.
Her hands define graceful shapes in the air. There is the
feel, the broken rhythm of a motor that won't catch. At
last, making a face of mock despair, she speaks a whir of
Danish, ends with a peremptory circle of her right hand.
"Tell her," she says in English, and relaxes back, smiling
and nodding, while Birte, smiling, translates for the
bride.

I am attentive. I care very much that I should be liked. I
smile at anyone who looks at me. The smallest polite-
ness enlarges in my grateful consideration. I say Thank
you when I mean to say Good evening.

Birte's exposition translates a graceful Danish to an
abrupt English.

"She says how could your mother have let you go so far
away with a man you only knew for two weeks?"

It could have been said many ways. Fru Raasloff has
perhaps said it differently. This is the way Birte will
always say it.

Muddled by my new sister-in-law's meanness, I answer

that my mother trusted my judgment.
"He looks to be trustworthy," Axel's father says in
English.
They all look at Axel. Pale blue eyes. Cheerful smile.
They all believe that a mother might trust him.
"Love will find a way," Axel's father adds.
Fru Raasloff smiles fondly at her son and at his young
wife.
The moment is past.

It seems that I am a novelty. So young a bride to not be
pregnant.
In Denmark, they tell me, no one marries younger than
twenty-five without special permission from the King.
He always grants permission when asked.
Everyone knows what the king's permission means.
Sour-faced Gena's marriage and first child came under
Royal auspices.
Eight years of marriage and a second child have not re-
deemed Gena's professor/husband in the eyes of her
family.
"So foolish! to get a girl pregnant!"
And now they are proven right.

Gena's domestic collapse has provided us with a house
of our own, a honeymoon cottage.
We bicycle the two miles between the houses.
We eat and bathe and visit with the family in the family
home.
We sleep and wake and have some privacy in the limbo
of this house that will be disposed of according to the
divorce decree.
Yellow-stuccoed, two stories high, it sits off on its own
road, as bleak in this Danish winter as the regulated
hatred it has held.
There have been no passionate arguments in these

rooms.

They reek of dry-eyed endurance.

Only the study, exorcised by walls of books, can be sat in.

I sit, hugging my chest, overheating the round-bellied stove with blocks of pressed peat, watching the cast-iron fire to a glow.

On the other side of the wall, unseen, the paint blisters away, flaking off the wall in protest.

• • •

"Jørn says that you let him come into the bathroom when you were naked in the tub."

It is Gena who speaks.

The smell is food and waxed furniture.

We are all at lunch.

The dining table is covered by a heavy linen cloth.

Between the table and the kitchen Armandine moves in a clean white apron.

Armandine's apron is starched so stiff that it will crack like thin white stone and shatter but it will never wrinkle.

Foolish!

Foolish and mistaken.

Axel has told me that they all swim naked in the summer and I have taken that for an ease with nakedness. Now it seems in this instant of all their faces turned toward me that the ocean allows nakedness and the bathtub is taboo.

"He knocked to say he had left something. I said he could get it."

Gena is smiling a tight lipped smile. Another pin put in.
"She thinks I'm a fool," I think.

I have never darned a sock.
"What do you do when socks have holes in them?"
"We throw them away."
Now they must question the wife Axel has brought
home, an American wife after all, who has never darned
a sock.
"They are cheap. We buy new ones."
"She means cotton," Axel says, "and nylon. It is warmer
there."

After dinner Fru Raasloff brings out her basket of wools,
places it between us and begins to teach me. I'm reassured and cozy in the rightness of it.
I mean to have a different life.
I also feel it is a proper bride's occupation, learning to
darn socks.
The family eases back.

There is a party where the bride wears a bride's dress, white and sheer chiffon with long sleeves falling in soft folds to a narrow band at the wrists. Draping folds over the breast catch to a wider band at the waist. A full skirt falls in soft pleats to the floor.

She wears a small pin of blood-red garnets, a gift from Fru Raasloff.

"I have worn it many years," Fru Raasloff tells her. And as if they have a secret, "My daughters . . . it would not suit them. It will suit you exactly."

The bride wears the pin on a thin velvet ribbon around her neck.

The two ugly sisters, when she is near, cannot keep their hateful eyes off the red garnets on the black ribbon on the white skin.

Axel wears a dark blue suit, a white shirt, a red bow-tie, a satisfied expression.

He raises his glass to toast his young wife across the table.

Before-dinner drinks, beer and schnapps on the table, wine, champagne, brandy, liqueurs: it is a traditional and acceptable drunken celebration with speeches and toasts. One fattish man serves as the classic obscene guest. He no sooner sits than he lurches again to his feet to make another toast in Danish. The table roars. He is taken for wonderful. The groom's first wife is there with her fiancé and takes the look of a martyr when her husband-to-be reaches over and grabs at her breast. He is glaring at Axel.

Fru Raasloff speaks down the table to a young man, the son of her first husband by his second wife: "On your father's deathbed," she tells him, "he said that I was the only woman he ever really loved."

The fat guest rises with his latest toast.

Fru Raasloff rises also.

At her back her chair tilts and crashes to the floor.
Carrying her wineglass, carried by her emotion, Fru
Raasloff comes around the table, walks the length of the
table smiling and in a dream. The bride rises, to be
caught in a tearful embrace.
"Welcome to our family!" Fru Raasloff cries out in English.
Her champagne pours down the younger woman's
back.

For dessert there are thin pastry cornucopias filled and
spilling sweet red berries. There is cream whipped as
thick as butter in a large crystal bowl and, to lift it out, a
heavily patterned silver spoon.

London

The night-boat from Denmark to England gleamed: polished brass and waxed wood; dark red carpeting underfoot; excellent food.
"How well you speak the language," Axel was told by an Englishman.
"I'm Danish," he replied, glowing; a compounded compliment.

From the night-boat to the boat-train and Liverpool Street Station.
Slimed cement, mucky with train-station dirt; thin slop squished in bubbles around Axel's sponge-rubber soles. We walked along the train to reach the front and be off the tracks.
Overhead, a high sloped roof, grimed-over windows let through a filtered gray light in angled widening bars, to the interior far below.

War sucks color out.
Gray faces. Gray hats. Gray mouths. Eyes gone grim.

War and rationing. A deep harsh winter. Outside the sky was gray, darkened by the drizzling slant of rain. The faces we passed were a fish-white pallor in the air's thin water.

It would be lovely to have style superior to every occasion.
We had no such hope. Oddments of luggage and over-stuffed paper bags. Three dozen eggs from Denmark and a huge chunk of cheese. We moved down the platform and through the station and into the street like a history of immigrants. I hung back against a wall, my fingers cramped and fixed through strings that held parcels of paper that couldn't be put on the wet sidewalk.

Axel was one more pale stranger moving back and forth along the curbing, ghostly, his right arm raised in a dancer's curve over his head. The isolated and predictable dance of a man who hails a cab in the rain.

War is a monstrous mouth.
London had great bites eaten away, whole city blocks gone in a bite. The rubble was cleared away. Wallpaper and fireplaces floated up the sides of buildings that still stood.
Doors opened into the third floor, the fifth floor, as many floors as there were. No more fires. No more rooms on this side to be entered into. All those stories of happy-home got stopped.

Axel's act of passion had cost him Africa, temporarily. His courtship and honeymoon had caused him to so overstay his six-months' leave that someone else had been sent in his place. Now he had to stay and work in London for at least a year, possibly two.

Mr. Collins invited us to dinner.

Mr. Collins was long-boned and gawky. His lack of grace seemed to be some kind of English value. It also seemed to be a value that he spoke as if he had strings pulling out on the corners of his mouth, flattening his words. It was a Mayfair accent, Axel told me.

Mr. Collins parted his hair in the middle so it stood over his forehead in a wiry kink of wings, a V that pointed down to a large nose and a horsey jaw.

Mr. Collins's sitting room was cozy with drawn drapes and lamps sitting in warm circles of light. A small fire glowed red in the fireplace. On the mantlepiece were the curves of three elephant tusks. They were carved into three safaris of ivory elephants in single file.

The walls had hangings of patterned blue and white cotton to match the drawn drapes.

"Nigerian," Mr. Collins told me, seeing me looking, "handwoven native."

Ostrich eggs held by red and blue strips of leather cut into patterns hung in a cluster next to the fireplace.

Between the fireplace and the couch where I sat with Mr. Collins was a small table that held my after-dinner coffee and a tiny brass figure of a man balanced on a round platform the size of a silver dollar. Long brass wires curved out and down from his shoulders to hold the weights that balanced him and caused him to stand on the single pinpoint of his feet.

"Toy," Mr. Collins told me and reached to touch one of the wires.

The small man careened and spun in a circle.

The base of the table that held the toy and the coffee had once been an elephant's foot and a piece of its leg. The toenails gleamed and the wrinkled skin was tanned leather. That table had died, been tanned and cleaned, been stuffed and had its toenails polished.

"How did Axel persuade you to come away so quickly?" one of the adjacent ladies asked me.

"I decided to come when he told my mother that he understood that she must feel upset at the two of us not knowing each other and asked whether it would reassure her for the two of us to have a trial marriage for a year and then make up our minds."

"Extraordinary," the lady drawled. "And what did your mother say?"

"She said that wouldn't exactly reassure her."

"Charming," the lady laughed. The lady looked me over.

All the guests were old Africa hands and spoke knowingly. Number-one boy. Government House. Up-country. Exotic phrases rose and sank with the regularity of crocodiles in a Tarzan movie.

I reached for my coffee, lifted my cup from the table that had taken its last walk.

Spring would return. We both believed it.
To live by the Heath and walk out onto rough grass
when the weather allowed would be nice, we thought.

With memories and a belief in Springs to come and the
cold wind blowing fog through our bones we went to
meander the hilly streets of Hampstead on the lookout
for uncurtained windows that held no cats, no birds, no
potted plants.

Buildings smashed flat by war had left too many people
to fill what was left standing. We walked block after
block and found nothing.
A grocer's window acted as a bulletin board and there
was a filing card there that advertised "Garden Flat With
Kitchen".
I thought of tulips as we walked along the street reading
the numbers and arrived at an old brownstone with a
cat, languid and elegant, looking out of the downstairs
window.
The front door was a monstrosity of colored glass made
into a pattern of triangles and diamonds and swung
open instantly when we rang the bell as if the woman
who opened it had been watching us come along the
street.

She was fat with small piggy eyes and rice powder wiped
over her face as if snow had fallen. She wore a linty
hairnet made of hair over round curls pinned in place
days earlier. Her plum velvet dress had a settled pattern
of wrinkles with the nap worn away at the upper curve
of the ridges. The V-neck was edged with scraggy fur
and she wore dirty wine houseslippers with scraggy fur
pompoms. Three cats of much the same sort of fur
wound around her feet and looked up at us with no
curiosity.

No, the flat had not been taken and she would be pleased to show it to us.

"It's a perfect place for a painter," she said as she led us along a narrow, dark hall which she referred to as ours. "This is your hall here. Then you go down these steps. And this is your door," which she opened onto a large basement room, low-ceilinged and square-shaped. One whole wall was covered by a large furnace and a maze of piping that disappeared up into the ceiling. The wall opposite held blue shelving with upright blue and white plates as décor.

The "kitchen" was a walk-in closet with no windows, lighted by a bulb that hung down on a ratty electric wire. A hotplate was on a shelf. The washingup could be done in the bathroom, or water could be brought from the bathroom in an enamel pan.

The "garden" was a sooty bit of cemented yard where all the dustbins for the house were kept.

"Is this the furnace for the house?" Axel asked.

It was, and a man must come in to stoke it unless we'd like to stoke it ourselves for a lower rent.

A grand piano filled one corner of the room and must be left there.

The landlady had no idea of how it had been got in and no notion of how to get it out.

"It was here when I bought the place and it'll be here when I sell it. If I sell it."

We already knew it was not possible, this perfect happy nightmare of "the artist's life," with the stoker in and out and the untuned piano, but we went through with the rest of the tour.

We would share the bathroom with the lady who was our guide, her slippers flip-flopping and ourselves following after. "Your bathroom," she called it, and the three of us stood solemnly looking at the porcelain fixtures while she explained that the curtains around the cast-iron tub were for the privacy of the tenants, who were expected to leave the door unlocked when they bathed as this was the only way into a part of the landlady's "suite". She delicately implied that we might lock the doors when we must use the "other convenience".

"Of course, when I know someone's bathing I don't go through unless I really must."

It was impossible, looking back into her little eyes fringed with rice powder, to know quite what that might mean.

We saw other, less artistic rooms in other parts of London and settled for a bed-sitting room in West Hampstead with two single-bed couches, a small sink with cold water, a sixpence-metered gas heater with a burner attached for cooking so near the floor that I sat cross-legged on the worn rug holding the off-center frying pan, if its contents were lightweight, to keep it from dumping onto the floor.

We shared a "water-closet" and a bath where, in privacy, one might drop a shilling into the geyser and have it explode in an open flame for a set number of minutes while the tub filled.

A young couple owned the house. The wife was very pregnant and her mother protected her daughter's interests, prowling the halls endlessly, suspicious and hard-faced.

Against this English winter my Danish father-in-law had given me two pair of long underwear, laughing when I insisted I could use them. One more charming Americanism. And it was true I needed them, having almost no warm clothing.

I wore my long underwear daily to the Slade where I still meant to learn to be a painter.

Over the long underwear I wore woolen stockings, denim Levi's, an itchy dark-blue wool weater got from Army/Navy Surplus where I had also got the smallest size of parachute trooper's boots.

Over all I wore an old sheepskin coat of Axel's.

It was warm and practical and markedly strange for London in 1950.

I stopped in Harrod's to buy a lipstick and a middle-aged Englishwoman passed me in the aisle, walked on another five feet and stopped, turned, looked at me with all the drama of a stage whisper from my neck down to the boots and back up again to the neck; turned to walk another three feet, turned back and did it all again.

And at a bakery near Knightsbridge Station a woman was leaving at the same instant I was arriving. Instead of the usual mutual move to the left and to the right the woman froze dead-center and said coldly, "Will you please move out of my way."

And I moved out of her way.

Hampstead Heath had hills, uncut wild grasses, stands
of trees, a brook, a real sky. It was very like being in the
country. People flew kites there on a high hill, children
with small paper-covered homemade jobs and a roughly
wound ball of string claimed equal rights with kites of
progressive splendor up to the grown man who flew a
giant contraption from a harness fitted around his body.
On windy days he would be jerked around and leaned
the whole weight of his body against the tug of a small
cable which came from the pit of his stomach to disappear in a slow curve into the sky. His kite when sighted
would be far to the left or right of where the cable disappeared.

Axel and I came up out of the ground at Hampstead
Heath Station, turned right to walk up the hill, then left,
looking to locate the house number Hans had given me.
This occasion was a picnic to meet Hans's new wife.
"She is like a Rubens!"
In the basket Axel carried were devilled eggs, potato
salad, and a loaf of hard crusted bread with a sharp
knife.

The hallway was dark as was the bed-sitting room. But
the kitchen was white and yellow with potted plants on
the wide sill of a large window. The day's lucky sunlight,
perfect for a picnic, poured through the plants and was
faintly tinged by them with a green that reflected on the
white walls.

The flat belonged to Hans. (Where did he paint, I wondered.) And now was clearly the place where he kept his
lady. Her garments were in little piles here and there,
the bed unmade. Some things were shoved under the
bed and the couch.
Passion?

It was true Alice was well-rounded, though small. Blond hair, very blue eyes, the look of her was emphasized by standing alongside Hans.

She ignored me after the introductions had been made and began to talk to Axel about how she wanted to travel.

"Life is so dull," she said.

"One must make amusements for oneself," she said in an affected, vivacious voice.

"I mean to travel. I'm not going to spend my life . . ." her voice faded. "I need clothes!" she interrupted herself to say to Hans, who sat quiet and miserable.

"I used to go to parties," and she began to name large hotels.

She would put on her party clothes, go to a hotel and take the elevator to the top floor. Then she would walk the length of the hall looking for a party. If there was no party on that floor she would go down to the next.

"There's always a party somewhere."

She knew where the most expensive suites in the hotels were and she'd try there first.

"They never know who all the women are. They might know the men but they never know all the women."

"Didn't anyone ever know you hadn't been asked," I asked.

"Oh, a few times. I said I was meeting my boyfriend there and I'd forgotten the room number but I was sure this was the floor."

Alice moved her chair closer to Axel and smiled at him. "I want to go to Paris. And Italy. And," archly as if now he could invite her, "I think I'd like Scandinavia. What's Denmark like?"

She turned her head, looking through Hans as if he weren't there.

"I love men with blond hair. I love blue eyes."

I thought we must have interrupted a quarrel that was
continuing in this oblique fashion.
"We should get outdoors," I said to the other three.
"We can talk outdoors," I insisted.

Axel went to the bathroom.
Hans and Alice and I sat around the small table under
the window waiting for him to return. Alice stopped
talking when Axel wasn't there. I tried to make conversation but Hans was sunk in sadness and Alice wouldn't
look at me so I stopped.
I watched the sun in the leaves, the sun we weren't out
in. It was as rare and precious as gold.
I dreamed into the light and the leaves it shone through.
As if my name had been spoken I came to myself in the
awkwardness of how long Axel had been gone.
I looked at Alice but Alice was staring hatefully at Hans.
I looked at Hans to find he had been watching me. His
face was melting and tender and I blushed. The heat
rose into my face.
Now Alice was looking at me, glaring with resentment.

Axel's return changed Alice's face utterly and she was a
charming good-time girl again, all for him.
The small apartment and Hans were nothing compared
to the good times she had known and would know
again and the charms of this stranger.

We left carrying two hampers, the heath a short walk
downhill past neighborhood shops, greengrocer, baker,
fishmonger, art supplies.

We crossed the street at the corner and walked into the
hills of grass. We passed the pond where children were

sailing boats, setting the sails on the windward side of the pond and running a half circle to stand waiting while the small craft would make its way across, curving and dipping in every breeze. Or would founder in the center, sails wrong, until someone would take a long stick and poke the small boat toward a waiting hand.

It was a warm day. A light breeze blew warm.

For a time we walked alongside a rough gully hearing the soft spring sound of water running along the bottom, through a tangle of fresh greening brush.
We came to a straggling stop in tall grass on a hillside.
We trampled around to make a nest and sat in our clearing surrounded by the grass left standing.
Nothing was simple.

Alice chattered compulsively leaving something unsaid. There continued to be the feeling, a stain on the time, that something was being left unsaid despite Alice's obvious intention to tell Axel everything.
He looked, she said, exactly like her first lover, also blond, also blue-eyed. Hans, it was increasingly clear, looked very different.

"The potato salad and the eggs are the way my mother made them," Hans said to me.
Alice talked faster. She began to talk about the Slade, where Hans and I were students. She implied that we "met" there. Which we did. And went for coffee together. And laughed together when the model, who was a week into a month-long pose, went for a weekend to Brighton and came in Monday morning a fiery red, her bikini stripings laid onto her torso forever insofar as this pose was concerned. And in one fell swoop all the carefully prepared palettes counted for naught.

But we did not "meet" there.

Still I was confused.
Did Hans think we "met" there?
No, I could not have so misunderstood him.
When he told me of his new wife he was happy.
Had he simply been hysterical?

The afternoon ended.
The time came for Axel and me to return to the station.
Alice and Hans walked us there.
Alice, walking ahead with Axel, still talked, describing
herself as passionate, sensual, as having the attributes of
women who only enjoy making love if the men are
blond with blue eyes.
Hans and I, the dark ones, walked behind, quiet.

At the station Alice insisted that Axel should buy three
tickets.
She meant to come along with us.
"I love you," she said, reaching for Axel's hand.
"I want to go with you."

We stood on the darkening platform missing our train
again and again while Alice played the beleaguered
heroine to whatever transient audience passed by.
Hans reasoned with her, begged, humored, nothing
would serve.
At last Hans held Alice forcibly while she screamed,
"Don't touch me!" And at last we boarded a train.
Hissings and crashing metal.
Lights came on on the platform just before the train
moved past the drama of Hans struggling with his Ru-
benesque wife, her arms flailing, mouth twisting.
And in the face, eyes clear and cold as decision. She had
decided not to stay.

As the train entered the dark tunnel I no longer saw Hans and Alice but saw the vivid reflection of myself and Axel against the dark glass.

I looked at Axel's reflected face.

Bits of what passed in the world outside shot past and along his face with no impact. He rested back from his ordeal with his eyes closed.

"It would have been wiser not to kiss her," I said to the reflection.

"Of course it would have been wiser after the fact! How was I to know she was a raving maniac? I just took her to be a girl who wanted to be kissed back of a bush and I did it!"

I said no more.

He seemed so right.

But there was something wrong in it, even so.

I wanted nothing more than I wanted to be in the
bathroom vomiting.
My mouth was covered with my hand to hold it in.
I gulped at Birte, who had telephoned.
"Birte . . . I've got to go . . ."
"We'll be eating at seven-thirty but you should plan to
arrive an hour before that."
"Birte . . . Axel will call you. I have to go now. I have to
vomit."

"And two weeks ago when there weren't enough chairs
Birte feels that you could have made a point of
standing."
"What else?"
"She says you didn't thank her for the invitation."

• • •

My parachute trooper's boots were as good as any to
start the waddling way toward motherhood.

"Will you be having a doctor or a midwife?"
"A *midwife*? I can choose a doctor or a *midwife*?"
(Visions of a New Mexican neighbor who assisted "at
home", taking a three-pound package of new lard when
she went. "She takes handfuls of it and crams it up when
the baby's coming to help it slide out." "She opens a
Bible and puts it under the pillow to keep the mother
and the baby safe." "She opens a pair of scissors and puts
them under the bed to cut the pain.")
The clinic nurse was Irish, a soft lilt to her questions.
"Do you mean to have the baby at home or in a
hospital?"
"In a hospital. I want to have the baby in a hospital."
Looking down at the form on her desk, pen poised, the
nurse asked, "First pregnancy?"

"Yes."

"Wait in there please. They'll call you."

She looked up, smiling, tipped her head to show where I must wait.

I was given an extra half-ration book and the right to buy a quart of milk a day for tuppence ha'penny. I went regularly to the clinic for powdered orange juice and vitamins and to have my pelvis measured with calipers. I liked having the extra bit of bacon, the extra bit of cheese, the extra bit of meat, the one more egg a week. My half-ration book announced my pregnancy in all the shops I regularly used. I could also buy bananas, when there were any, along with old people over sixty and children under twelve.

In August, when I was six months pregnant, we went for a weekend at Brighton. We stayed at a bed-and-breakfast. Breakfast was a badly cooked egg, half a tomato semi-cooked under a broiler, and two pieces of fried bread. I wore my old bathing suit on the beach. It fitted except for the extra bulge in my breasts and a smallish potbelly.

The next month I blossomed into an enormous round of myself and someone else lodged on the shelf of hip bones.

We were not going to Africa at all.

We were going to the Caribbean for someone entirely different.

• • •

The colony was to be improved by the addition of a tourist hotel.

The hotel would not be palatial but its modesty was to be compensated for by services. An abundance of cheap labor is the traditional natural resource and commodity

of under-developed countries. Servants would light cig-
arettes, shine shoes, care for small children, hand-
launder clothing, carry breakfast trays to bedrooms and
private verandas.

It was thought that the hotel might begin to attract a
small share of the Caribbean tourist boom to the colony, now a poor and pathetic place with only lobsters
for an export.

The plans for the hotel were made and drawn up in
London in a government office by a civil servant who
had never been out of England. The necessary data was
available on paper. The guidelines were printed in a
small booklet. The quondam architect used a map and a
note on prevailing winds and the job was soon done.

The plans were copied in as many blueprints as would
be needed; groundwork for limitless misunderstanding
in time and space.
The mistakes, often grotesque, would occur at the other
end and return to London as more paperwork to be
solved on paper.

Various departments of the Colonial Development Corporation were activated by the plans. Bar stools and concrete and steel beams were ordered to be shipped. A
wide range of skilled and semi-skilled labor was hired. A
hotel manager was hired prematurely and would arrive
to find himself with two years of salary and no hotel to
manage.

Like a single handful of rice thrown onto the city from
high overhead, the powers activated a small scatter of
making ready.
Passports were renewed. The clothing allowances

granted according to rank were spent. Passages were booked.

One Tuesday as a part of this sanctioned activity an order was being placed with a Bond Street tailor for two blue suits to be made up in tropic-weight wool.

The person bending his arms and legs to be measured was Axel Raasloff recently hired by the Colonial Development Corporation to be the resident architect during the hotel's building.

The tailor, thin-faced and expressionless, elegant, would murmur in Axel's ear and Axel would hold a limb at an awkward angle while a yellow tape was spanned between one crucial point and another.

I sat, twenty and very pregnant, in a soft chair, a small table with an emptied teacup and saucer at my side, and watched the suits be invented into the air around Axel's slim figure.

The style of the occasion was impressive. A Bond Street tailor is no mean thing to see. A gesture of his hand created the fall the coat would have. A pinching turn of the thumb and forefinger showed where the trousers would hold a pleat.

Axel rose to the occasion. He demonstrated a settled taste in the cut a lapel should have and chose the dark blue he had hoped to find.

I watched in a daze of well-being. The soft chair, the tea, the murmur of voices beguiled my senses. I loved the slight smell of new cloth. I bathed in the atmosphere of new cloth. I could believe it now that we would leave London with its consistently unseasonable weather. We

would go by ship to warm water and sunshine. Island
beaches and palm trees unfolded forward in time from
the London tailor's shop in an infinity of picture postcards. From this moment we were enroute to the tropics
and to the house being prepared for us there.
I would be slim again in that place and wear cotton
dresses with my arms bare and brown and dance with
Axel in one of his new suits at the Club he had told me
would be there.
We would swim in warm salty water. Calypso music
and moonlight.

At last the tailor brushed his client over with a soft
bristle brush as if to dispel the touching. A few platitudes
floated in the air to conclude the ritual.

Dazed with care and special attention, we went down a
flight of stairs and were reclaimed by reality. A quick
sharp wind chilled any inch of flesh that wasn't covered.
Axel tightened his wool scarf and I buttoned the small
very top button on my coat. The day was predictably
gray, the sun long since covered over with no hope of
return.

At a Lyons Corner House we turned in through the
door.
The warm air made our faces feel stiff. Our ears and
cheeks had turned red in the short distance we had
walked. Axel pulled the clean handkerchief he always
carried from his pocket to wipe his eyes and nose.
"Just the blue I wanted."

We surveyed the cart of fancy pastries as if we surveyed
our altered prospects, slightly larger than life-size.
We celebrated the imagination of our future with fancy
pastry and a shared pot of steaming tea.

Jamaica

In dreams I'm in a small room and the ship is sinking.
I'm running for the door as the floor beyond it rises like
a water level.
The opening is disappearing as I'm running toward it.
I must climb to reach it, clinging to the upper door jamb
with the tips of my fingers.
All the while people are screaming where I can't see
them.

• • •

We went up the gangplank. The gangplank was steady.
It was another winter departure.
Our cabin was larger, more comfortable. Our luggage
was already there.
Tea and drinks were in the upper lounge. Lunch would
wait for the sailing.

Axel wrote our names in for the second sitting in the dining room. It's how one avoids the children.

Another cold deck, slippery with rain and it was England we were leaving now.
Pigeons. Sparrows. Black-headed gulls. Swans on the Thames.
Ravens at the Tower of London. Massed flights of starlings.
Hampstead Heath. Kew at lilac time. Hans with his shrieking wife.
Chiffon gowns in the windows at Harrod's.
Goodbye.
Goodbye.

Children racketed but the adults were mostly silent.
And the island was left.
No one stayed to watch it to the last. They'd all gone to lunch.
To the dining room rich with flowers and stiff shining linen.
To butter. Sugar. Menus with a choice.
I was embarrassed to feel a rush of emotion at the sight of so much food.
"One good meal and I can't believe in suffering."

The first three mornings I ate a double breakfast.
Orange juice and buttered toast and scrambled eggs, and sausages, and good coffee and sweet jams and marmalade.
Axel raised his eyebrows.
"Have you begun to eat for triplets, my dear?"
It was true I was burgeoning.
In that sudden dump outward women sometimes achieve in the last month of pregnancy my body had become as unwieldy as if I carried a permanent piece of

furniture. Overstuffed. It rocked me back on my heels, turned my toes out in a waddle, and curved my backbone.

When the stewardess caught sight of me her eyes widened and she came to ask me specific questions. Someone had made a mistake. A woman three weeks away from delivery should never have been allowed onto the ocean! Not on a ship *she* had any say over. It was clear that I had been saved by my tent of a coat. If the stewardess had a choice in it I would be put in one of the rowboats, pointed toward England and left to my own resources.

I saw the stewardess and the ship's doctor in grim conversation looking at me. A part of the conversation must be the extent to which I was not following the stewardess's advice to spend as much time as possible in bed. "I feel fine!" I insisted and saw her not be pleased. To the stewardess it was as she had feared. If there was to be any sensible worrying done it must all be done by herself. The price one pays for authority.

Warmer waters and sunshine egged me on. I was given the use of a bathing suit by a friendly fat woman. It was a wrap-around of cotton. I tied myself into it daily and went into the pool. Some of the more traditional-minded adults on board made it clear that I should be decently hiding myself away but I had the advantage of being badly brought up and would not notice them. I came in second in Ladies Shuffleboard but did badly at partnered quoits despite being paired with a real athlete. My partner was a man named Valentine who was one of the two bowlers for the Jamaican cricket team and was on his way home after having achieved, with the

others, a victory the month before at Lords, where they
had beaten England.

Lord Kitchener and Lord Beginner had written instant
calypsos in honor of the victory.

"Those two little friends of mine
Ramadin and Valentine," went one of them. And here
was the great Valentine himself, six feet four or five, thin
as a rail, black as black, gentle and shy. He was the sort
of man who must smile at his shoe and agree when the
deck-games lady insisted.

Valentine and I made an incongruous pair.

"You look like a ball and bat," Axel told me.

A hurricane was in the vicinity and made the ship
wallow the last day before its arrival in Kingston.

I was sitting in the upper lounge when the ship took one
particularly high wave and every chair in the room with
its back four-square to the downhill side fell over, in-
cluding mine.

Axel and the stewardess were at my side before I could
stand.

I lay on the floor laughing.

● ● ●

One thing made clear to me in the past year was that I
had married a ladies' man. Whenever Axel went to help
the hostess in the kitchen she would reappear with
heightened color and a jollier disposition.

Axel thought of it as if he raised the value of the time
passed. As if he were a social resource. As if he ranked
along with the music and the drink.

I never thought the moon was made of green cheese,
but then however much that's used to show an indecent
credulity I was never *really* encouraged to believe it.

I was, on the other hand, encouraged by persons as di-
verse as Pearl Buck and Elsa Lanchester to believe that a
man's sexual adrenalin deserves a support system.

Pearl Buck's books were all I would find to read when
we would visit my grandmother in Santa Fe. Pearl Buck
had a variety of wonderful Number-One wives, each
without flaw. In some instances it was wife Number-
One who chose her husband's wife Number-Two,
making sure that the younger woman would have a gentle disposition and sweet breath.

Elsa Lanchester was a society wife in a movie that glit-
tered with cloth and jewels and attitudes. She told her
friends that she couldn't bear Reggie when he didn't
have a nice little flirtation going. He became too dull to
talk to and spoiled the look of the furniture.

In all the instances of these broad-minded women they
were only shown as charming and they were always the
most important woman present.

My own father would hit my mother with his fist whenever he wanted to; and when he had girlfriends my
mother suffered.

There was no doubt that Elsa Lanchester had it better.

Axel directed his interest toward the woman who sat in
a deck chair on the other side of my belly.

"Of course I love you!" she had just snapped at the small
girl who had come away from her toys to whisper in her
mother's ear.

The child shrank back from the anger in the woman's
voice and returned to shoving her toys about in a lack-
luster fashion. To please her mother the child pretended
to play.

"If I had *known* what a nuisance she would be without
her nurse . . . !"

The mother rolled her eyes up to show us that she had

suffered.

"You live in Jamaica?" Axel asked then.

"Yes," she smiled and was delighted to tell him, preening, that she and her husband owned such-and-such a resort in Montego Bay.

Axel's charm blossomed. And bore fruit.

"She wants us to visit," he told me after a turn around the deck with the lady in question while I and my book stayed at the deck chairs with the child and her toys.

Mrs. MacNeil had disappeared with her child to her appointment at the beauty salon below decks.

Now that her boredom was relieved by the presence of an attentive man she dazzled the other passengers nightly with a show of her various wardrobe and spent a piece of most afternoons laid up in the beauty salon for repairs and improvement.

The small girl also benefited by the woman's improved circumstance. She got an occasional pat and a smile. If she misjudged her mother's brief caress and clung to her the woman would recoil in a disgust equal to the child's longing.

"She is *so* demanding!" The child would be shoved away.

During a desultory conversation the day before we were due to arrive Axel made the mistake that caused the lady to stop payment on his plans.

We were discussing whether it was cheaper for men or for women in their student years. Axel felt strongly that women were benefited by being taken to dinner by men.

"It might not be the case for unattractive women but any young woman with looks can count on getting a few free meals a week."

Mrs. MacNeil was concerned that we should both know she had also roughed it in her student days. "When I was a student I lived on . . ." and she named some small amount, ". . . a week."

"That's my point exactly," Axel pounced, "and you were taken to dinner by your men friends!"

"Well, yes," she acknowledged.

"You could live that cheaply because you had your youth and good looks!" Axel said in triumph.

Mrs. MacNeil, freshly coiffed and draped round with peach chiffon to show off her figure, went frigid. She looked at Axel, who only knew he had made his point, and said "Well!"

"You said, 'that's when you *had* your *youth* and *good looks*,'" I explained, amazed that he still didn't understand what he had done.

"And so she had! That's why she could live so cheaply," he continued to insist.

• • •

The Caribbean is a deep valley with mountains that rise from the ocean floor to become Cuba, Haiti, Puerto Rico, a beaded line of the Bahamas, and Jamaica.

The ship sailed routinely among and through these mountain peaks, through the Windward Passage with Cuba closer on the right than Haiti, far off on the left, and continued dead straight for Jamaica, vivid green on a froth of lace where surf foamed.

Tropical air is a warm breathing, an intimacy, blind and nuzzling. it touches exposed skin with an unrelieved caress.

Valentine was not a man to swagger but his island home knew how to swagger for him, their own true darling. On the dock three steel bands were set up and played with no reference to each other. All the dock was filled with dancing people.

The passengers had been told that no one might disembark until Valentine had been welcomed by the Lord Mayor.

Valentine flashed brief smiles upward but spent most of the welcoming speech looking at his shoe. The dignitaries melted in the heat and the Lord Mayor of Kingston, dressed for the occasion in a purple wool gown with a heavy gold chain of office hanging around his neck, gave Valentine a large golden key and proclaimed a public holiday.

Axel continued to scan the decks. He meant to reconcile himself with Mrs. MacNeil but she was nowhere to be seen.

As space opened, the crowd followed after Valentine and his greeters, and the other passengers made their way down the gangway.

Axel was met by two young men from the Kingston office of the Colonial Development Corporation who had made reservations for us at a hotel in the hills above Kingston. We had the use of a small Ford Prefect during the four days we meant to stay.

Axel was to meet with his business associates on Thursday morning and our plane to Belize was to leave on Friday.

Hibiscus too thick to see through, twelve feet high. Grass-green, fine as a thread to the thickness of a pencil, the most elegant lizard — "Isn't it charming! Oh

look!"—caught and unmoving on the dining room wall
next to a window that is almost to the ceiling and almost
to the floor. No fear in that green shape against the
white wall.

And us: we move in keeping with the place. Our gestures are larger and more languid.
Ah, and the lizard is gone.

But it is raining a bit. And then it is raining more. And
then it is not raining but high up there are lumps of
cloud moving fast.
A warm breeze is blowing in gusts. At their worst the
gusts make the flowers rage and whip alongside the
road. When the gust is past, the sun drops in a leaden
thud from the sky.
It is a hurricane. Off there someplace there is a hurricane
swirling its gigantic circle and snaking its influence over
water . . . far enough away to give us only the side ef-
fects. So far.

"Hurricane."
"Hurricane?"
"Been around a couple of days now. Well off the island.
North and East. Bit of a blow because of it."
"Is it likely to swing around and come here?"
"Warning flag's up to show it's within fifty miles. If the
red flag goes up, that's when to head for cover. No real
danger in all likelihood."
"Ah."

Two days later in the continuing uneven weather,
drizzle and wind alternating with brilliant sunshine, we
drove in the tiny Ford Prefect through Kingston enroute to the northern side of the island.
Axel meant to show me Montego Bay without Mrs.

MacNeil's help.

Minutes after we had passed Government House the warning flag we hadn't noticed was lowered and a red flag was run up in its place.

Hurricane Lucille had changed her course and was moving toward Jamaica.

The car labored in its rise to three thousand feet above sea level. The windshield wipers were keyed to the engine. When the engine was not accelerating the wipers stopped. When we drove downhill, Axel had to open the car door and put his head out into the rain.

High up, at a view point, we stopped to look down into the valley. A lightning rod thirty feet away fulfilled its function. We were as shocked as if we had been hit. We were alive to register the shock. We made our way back to the car and continued on.

As we drove, the road was often awash with water and we drove into those washings with no sense of how deep they might be, trusting that the road was still there, out of eyesight.

We got to Tower Isle in the mid-afternoon. All the outdoors, the beach, the swimming pool, the outdoor dance floor, all was rain. To see what we had hoped for, we looked at the rack of picture postcards.

For company there were two couples of newlyweds on honeymoon who played canasta and told each other vivaciously about St. Louis, Missouri and Pocatello, Idaho.

All night the rain continued. The wind grew stronger, angling roughly, throwing the water in gusts by the bucket.

"The telephone wires are down," the desk clerk told us the next day, advising us against leaving the hotel. "Two touring busses that should have arrived this morning from Kingston have not come."

"If it gets too bad we'll come back," Axel answered.

"You do understand?" the desk clerk turned to me, giving up on Axel. "It is a hurricane."

"I have a business appointment tomorrow morning," Axel told him. "Our plane leaves day after tomorrow."

"I must advise you strongly against trying to cross the island," the clerk insisted.

"If it gets too bad we'll come back," Axel said again.

And with all the omnipotence of ignorance we left the hotel.

Axel had to drive with his head out of the door again. Again we crossed the lakes of water that crossed the road.

Until we didn't.

One lake we drove into simply rose and continued to rise. We sank into it.

When the water came through the floorboards Axel switched the engine and headlights off and called, "You take the wheel," to me.

He jumped out of the car and began to push. I reached across to steer. The car sank deeper into water. The water and mud was over my lap.

"Is the road washed away?" I yelled but couldn't be heard above the racket of the storm.

The water lay on the road for fifty feet. Somewhere along it the car began its uphill rise and rose out of its bath.

We stayed three days in a two-room cabin high on a hill over a sugar cane field.

The overseer for what had been a banana plantation but

was now a wreckage of cane and banana trees and floating dead chickens and livestock had found us at our tem-
porary lake and invited us home. He lived with his wife
and two children in the small house.

What had been a hill was now a small island.

The third day the water began to recede and a man rode
to the house on a bicycle to say that a car had come
through from the island's other side by driving the
coastal road.

We stopped twice and with others helped move a tree
from the road. The trees were still falling even though
the winds had passed. The landscape was ravaged, a
chaos of bits and breakage. Dead animals lay against
whatever barrier had stopped them.

The Kingston we returned to was changed.

Valentine had had his day and been blown off the front
page by accounts of the worst disaster to hit Jamaica in
fifty years.

All the crops were ruined. The fields were destroyed.

No planes could leave the island until the airstrips were
cleared.

Axel found himself with time enough for his business
meeting.

Another two days passed before we left.

Two photographs were taken of the mother-to-be during that week in Jamaica. The camera used was an old
Zeiss-Eikon that leaked light streaks through the
bellows.

In the first picture, taken the morning after arrival, it is
early and she is standing outside her bedroom on a
second-floor veranda. She is wearing a long nightgown
of thin white stuff. Her body is a shadow through the
cloth, a thin column swelling in the middle with the hid-

den presence of the unborn child. A slight breeze carries
the gown and holds it against her.
She is not awkward.
She is standing in sunlight, looking out and down onto
flowers.
Her body is an exquisite curving.

She saw a large expanse of clipped grass, its periphery
defined by a tall hedge of pinkish-red hibiscus, the
flower large with ragged edges and a single pistil, thin
and golden, protruding into the air. She saw an unused
fountain half-filled with a clutter of dry leaves and de-
bris. The metal pipe in the center was rusted and
dribbled a constant wavery bit of water. At night frogs
congregated in that dampness and sounded their racket.

In the later photograph, after the hurricane has turned
on its track and returned to wreck the island, she is at
the airport.
Now she is awkward, her bulk looking as if the storm
has left her stranded. She is frowning and tired.

Our next stop would be an arrival at our future.

In the Colony

The town is mainly flat, much of it on land reclaimed from swamp. It is cut into two parts by a narrow river which widens at its mouth into a bay, a natural harbor. Queen Street, the main street of the town, crosses the river with a metal bridge. A bridge is lifted twice during the day to let fishing boats go through. The first time at dawn when the boats must go out. The second time in the early evening when they return.

The houses are of two kinds with variations. The "local" house is small and square, one story near or on the ground, square holes for windows with solid flats of wood hinged at the top to be propped open in the daytime and closed at night with a latch. These houses are made of soft wood and often lean in the direction that is most eaten away. The second type of house is hardwood, painted white. It is two stories raised still higher on a foundation of stilts for more breeze and fewer mosquitoes. The high-pitched roof is corrugated tin painted red to slow the inevitable rust. Around the roof's edge is a tin gutter to catch rainfall. A pipe extends from the gutter to an enormous round water tank that sits in the yard as companion piece to the houses that can afford it. This second kind of house commands the major streets, the pleasant views, the sea breezes. This is the "backra" house where the white people live.

One of these houses with a small square of grass in front sat among others on the Foreshore. It faced, across a paved road, the ocean and the moorings of half a dozen small sailing boats owned by people who sailed for pleasure.
Quin Culpe, thin and boney, dressed in white kit for tennis at the club, wandered musing into the downstairs bedroom of his company-supplied home.
He wondered, as all do who like to cut it sharp, whether he might have asked for more money. He had asked for twice what they would have paid at the boarding house. Not too dear a price, he thought. Generous in fact for a man who loved his home and privacy. Generous of him to give up a bit of his well-loved home to strangers. A friend in need.
He stood in the uninteresting room to see it anew.
Perfectly adequate, he thought.
It occurred to him that he could ask for more money after the baby came. It would be more work for the cook and the maid. Bottles and nappies.
He sniffed a sniff with a nose as pointed as any bird that ever feathered its nest and went off on his two legs to his car.
He was proud of his legs.
He thought of himself as small but shapely.

Racquet and tennis balls were in the back seat and without any particular farewell to his wife, giving her no chance to remind him that today was the day for her

weekly visit to the prenatal clinic (My God! two pregnant women in one small house! Now *that* was above
and beyond the call of duty!) he climbed into his tidy
blue Morris Minor and reversed out of the driveway.
The walk would be good for her.
They must both stay fit.
He'd be the first to say that she should take a taxi, but he
knew that she would walk. He was an indulgent husband with a decently thrifty wife. He would chide her
for her little economies. She was never egged on by his
chiding to reckless expenditure.

In this tropical place the books will fall away from their
bindings if they are not taken regularly from their
shelves and exposed to light. Dark clothing must be
taken regularly from the closet and hung in the day's air
or it will develop splotches of mildew.
Shoes not worn regularly grow moss inside.

"Lice! Lice! Trow de bahl! Trow de bahl, Lice!"
Children are playing in a vacant lot near the Foreshore.
The girl named Lois throws the ball.

Water must be boiled, cooled and bottled for drinking.
Mosquito nets circle the beds.
The buzzards of this place, John Crow their local name,
wheel slowly through the hot skies on the lookout for
carrion.

Still, it would be strange (Quin Culpe drove around a
sleeping dog) to have foreigners in the house. God
knows what they might expect. Danes are notorious
feeders and all the world knows how Americans are.
Americans clamor in the marketplaces of the world,
buying, buying, greedy, voracious. They would ruin
him if they could.

He must be quite firm. They would find him a man to be reckoned with. Their standards would soar no higher than his well-ordered English household was prepared to sustain.

I looked at all that green smashed to garbage, poor little paradise.

The major news that morning had been how many nations were coming running with the green stuff that would kiss it and make it well.

The local plane, rattling and small, with one propeller, took us away from what would never be included in a tourist brochure.

Travel made me tired.
I wanted my body back.
I wanted to be the only person inside my skin.
I was at the end of my rope and we'd finally arrived at the beginning.

The Belize airport building shimmered in the heat to show it was apt to disappear, a plastered-over flat box with WELCOME TO BRITISH HONDURAS painted on the front.
Leaving the plane, walking on soft tar, the passengers shoved through solid heat on their energyless way to a door marked Immigration.
Past Immigration and Customs the building was cool.
We were handed iced fruit drinks by Mr. Sinclair as we left the railed enclosure.
We also met Mr. Culpe who moved constantly and never stopped smiling.
We all shook hands.
Mr. Sinclair had thick gray hair and freckles, was middle-aged, friendly. He arranged for our bags to be put in his car and we waited inside while it was being done.

The weekly plane from Jamaica and the weekly plane from New Orleans both arrived the same day; the first at 1:00 PM, the second at 3:00 PM. Anyone arriving or

leaving from the colony would be at the airport together
with whoever had come to say goodbye or hello or
both.

Rob Sinclair and Quin Culpe knew everyone. They
knew others who had arrived and those who had come
to meet them and knew the passengers checking their
bags for the return flight to Kingston and knew who was
waiting to meet whom on the New Orleans flight.

"Allan! Good to see you. You're on your way to the
States?"

Everyone here seemed to know everyone else's business.
And there were people who had simply come out for
the weekly party this all made.

"You know how it is in the tropics," Rob said over his
shoulder to Axel. The thin road was leading us out of
the airport past bushes of dusty hibiscus.

He meant that we had no house.

Axel agreed. Oh yes, he was all too well aware of how
plans and execution were at cross purposes in the
tropics.

"It might be as long as two months, but in the meantime
Quin and Mavis have offered to house you. The CDC
will pay for it."

"How generous of you," I said over my own shoulder to
Quin Culpe.

"It's nothing fancy but I think you'll be comfortable."

Some people move around the world like they're nor-
mal because that's what passes for human style but really
they're like black holes in the Universe. There's a
ravenous desire inside them that sucks and sucks and
can't ever be content. They can't bear anybody else's
reality.

Whatever and whoever comes into prolonged contact
with a neurotic runs the risk and likelihood of some

kind of transformation.

Ideally you see it in them, what they are, fast enough to let you go into rapid reverse and back out.

In this instance we didn't know Quin Culpe and we had been promised to him for a couple of months.

That's all. It wasn't forever. Just a couple of months.

"What hit me," people say, walking away in a daze after just five minutes with a potent neurotic.

Just a couple of months.

And that "couple of months" was the next plan in a system of plans that had already let us down. You know how it is in the tropics.

"MY DARLING ROSE," I said to Rob Sinclair, pointing. Between the airport and Belize the road was one lane of tartop. There were passing bays at regular intervals. The road went through lightweight jungle, walls of growth on both sides fifteen feet high; and through swamp where the water was the rich color of oil, and white lilies floated on the surface. Iguanas sunned on fallen logs. We would sometimes catch sight of an orchid, a sudden color, in the crotch of a tree far enough off the road so it hadn't fallen an easy prey to the passing traffic.

MY OWN
HEARTS DESIRE

The houses along the way to the town were named. The names were written in paint on board or on a rusting piece of corrugated tin, and nailed onto posts or trees near the road. The houses were shanties made of wood with a door and two windows. The names were a high-flown fancy. One, surrounded by flowers, leaning sideways, ready to fall, was MODERN TIMES.

On the outskirts of the town the shanties multiplied rapidly, became a swarming of wooden structures and half-
naked children and thin sick-looking dogs. A smell rose
from a nearby canal.
It was the place where the nighttime and maybe
daytime slop jars were emptied. When a pail was emptied there would be a swirl in the water.
If you didn't know and reached in you might well lose a
finger.

There was always the heat.
The ocean breezes never reached these back streets.
Children and chickens and dogs; one dog that had run
out of luck was a feast for half a dozen buzzards. They
racketed and hissed at each other but were too en-
grossed in feeding to fight. They hopped over and
around the ragged carcass with their wings out for
balance.
Ugly.
Ugly.

We swung right onto what Rob Sinclair said was Queen
Street, crossed a metal bridge. Passed the market.
The market was slow and bright with cloths stretched to
make shade over the fruits and vegetables and chilis.
We turned toward the foreshore and came, at last, on a
sweet ocean breeze that carried the smell of salt into the
car and cooled us.

"Not fancy, but I think you will find it comfortable."
Quin Culpe repeated his formula as we stood in the
center of a drab and barren room.
Ah, but the front window looked onto the ocean and
the boats moored there, and would show the sunset.
It *was* only two months.
"I'm sure we'll be comfortable," Axel reassured him.

Rob Sinclair looked the room over more critically. When he and his wife had come to dinner this had been the room where the guests had left their wraps. He distinctly remembered more furniture. There had been another bedside table, another lamp, a small desk with a straight chair. Some pictures, landscapes, fruit, something like that.

"If there's anything you need we can get it at the office. We've got the furniture, some of it, for your house. You can take any of it you'd like and then take it along with you when you leave."

He saw no point in pushing the issue.

Axel wanted a drafting table. He liked to bring work home. And yes, I'd like a soft chair. Something I could sit in next to the window when I wanted to sit and read.

Quin Culpe felt a revulsion at the instant demands until he remembered that he wanted the two of them to stay in their room as much as possible.

"Working evenings, eh?" he smiled approvingly. "You'll make the rest of us look like lay-abouts."

"Oh, Quin," his wife said breathlessly, "no one could think that about *you!* You're never home before six and you often go back."

Mrs. Culpe was Mavis. "Do call me Mavis!" she had insisted.

Mavis hovered in the doorway, perpetually on the verge of leaving the room. Her husband made no response to her endorsement.

"Is there a particular time of day for paying our respects at Government House?" Axel asked.

Quin Culpe stopped himself short of saying that as foreigners they would not be expected.

"Oh no. Anytime between ten and four. You'll meet Sir

Arthur's secretary, Mr. Niles. He'll have the book."
Quin Culpe thought Axel was being pushy.
The form was, one signed the book, then got asked to
dinner or at least to tea. Axel was simply asking to be
asked.

I wondered whether Quin Culpe might be shy with
strangers.
His wife certainly was, hanging in the doorway.
How could I know that in our host we had the town's
demon of the dance floor, the whirlwind of the tennis
courts, the prince of style.

Rob Sinclair invited the four of us to dinner the following night and left.
Mavis asked whether anyone would like tea.

"Heavenly Prospect," I answered, signs in my mind.

Roosters bring the day up, poor scrawny things to
sound so splendid. Before the first show of light their
racket begins. They excite each other to hysterical
effort. The dogs are also infected, that in the day's heat
will have as much as they can do to move from the sun
into the shade. They bark and howl until they feel
they've done enough.

Old Vivvy, wearing a dirty rainbow of dresses, goes into
Mrs. MacDougal's prized garden, a shadow among early
dawn shadows, to pick the flowers.
"When that woman was a child everything she touched
was gold!"
"When that woman was a child . . ." she owned the first
piano in the colony. Her parents meant to make her a
concert pianist. Both parents were killed in an accident
and the child's guardian took the money. That was the
story.
In the local voice, a calypso swing to her speech and
with the drawn out, pulled out rhythms of any story-
teller dealing with a myth, Rosa told me (later), "Whan
dhat whomahn wass a chile *ehverting* she touch wass
ghol!"
Who stands now in the palest gray lift of early morning
at Mrs. MacDougal's door, a mahogany door polished
to a high shine, and drops the brass knocker repeatedly
on its sounding brass panel until the door is opened a
cautious crack then wide by Mrs. MacDougal herself, in
a pink dressing gown, who looks in shock to see her
treasured darlings, all the flowers from her garden, in a
crushed mass, a madwoman's bouquet, held toward her
as Old Vivvy simpering says "Fi' cents?"
Mrs. MacDougal pays the five cents and brings her
fresh-picked flowers indoors, to the kitchen, where she
puts water in the sink and the flowers also. Flowers, she
would be the first to say, are best picked in the early

morning while dew still clings to the petals, as it does to
these.

Vivvy takes her five cents and turns down Queen Street
to go to the market.

In the gray light of pre-sunrise the fishing boats are still
arriving to unload. Donkey carts filled with small stringy
avocados, juiceless oranges, pineapples, breadfruit, plan-
tain, coconuts, are standing around in the bare yard. At
the yard's far end are boxes of wilted chickens. Iguanas
scuffle in the dirt, their front legs pulled like arms to be
tied behind their backs.

"Dey are de *bess* ting in de whorl to eat!" Rosa would insist to me who never, all the time I was there, did eat
one.

There is an inner building where half-carcasses hang,
blood dripping, and flies and cats go through the mesh
to feed on the meat.

Mrs. MacDougal leaves the flowers in the sink until
later and returns to her bed up the polished winding
staircase. Her house is graceful throughout, the advantage of her own and Gordon's taste. On the second floor
she passes the door to Gordon's bedroom, the door to
her dying husband's bedroom, and enters her own
bedroom, a feminine haven of imported goods.

She has a headache beginning that will last, probably, all
day, a fierce headache. All her flowers have been picked
and having them in the kitchen sink in the water is no
help at all.

The rising sun finds the day well under way in that small colony of houses.

"You gwan to cahtch you a husbahn foh suah, you keep lookin lahk dhat!" a woman almost hidden by trays of green and yellow chili peppers called out to Sally, the Culpe's cook, as she passed with her meager basket.

Sally's bad-temper was settled enough to not be relieved by the laughter around her, by the voices singing and calling over the large market space.

"Yes, indeed," another woman took up the joke and sang, "You wahnt to be happy an' live a king's life never make a pretty wohmahn your wife . . ."

Sour-faced Sally walked on past, down the long aisle of breadfruit and avocados, to the quayside where she bought a red snapper for dinner. Marketing would be even less a pleasure now. Mr. Culpe had made it clear that she would not have more money for the two extra lodgers.

She walked back through the shaded meat house and out through the poultry yard to Queen Street, turned left and left again and was on the cobbled road that ran along the Foreshore and would take her to her morning's work.

The roosters have crowed and stopped. The dogs have barked and stopped. Mrs. MacDougal is back in her bed asleep, a damp cloth on her forehead. Old Vivvy, having been raised to be clean, comes to the Fort Square seawall to bathe. The cast-off dresses she wears in layers of filthy faded print are laid over the wall.

Wearing, on different mornings, one dress or two or nothing at all, she goes into the water among the morning's slops.

Light pours horizontally over the flat still water and the day's heat begins.

On the Foreshore a battle had begun: the battle of the breakfast egg.

Quin Culpe had begun as he meant to continue.

"Fried bread and marmalade is perfectly adequate," he insisted to Sally, who stared resentfully at the floor.

"But Quin," Mavis Culpe quavered, hearing the echo of the notices given by all the cooks before this one, "we have *always* had eggs for breakfast!"

"There's no need for a feast at breakfast time!" Quin Culpe's eyes bulged with pressure.

His hair was glued to his head, the curl caught and held like a tightly plowed field above the fierce wrinkles on his forehead above the intent beak of his nose. If the world could only be held in place and controlled so simply.

"Our food bills have gone up!" he said to his wife.

He turned to the couple who must sit through this early morning tirade with a most inappropriate smile wavering on his mouth.

He meant them to see that he was not unreasonable.

"There've been many times in my life when I would have thought myself lucky to have had a cup of tea, much less fried bread and homemade jam!" He named off the items as if he named jewels.

We looked back at him, not to be fooled.

This breakfast time hysteria of Quin's had shocked us both.

"You know, Quin, we *can* stay at the boarding house. It would cost the CDC less money and we wouldn't be inconveniencing anyone."

Quin Culpe had counted on good manners. The manners his wife and daughter used quite normally in their dealings with him. It had not occurred to him that the

Raasloffs might simply leave if the situation didn't suit them.

Now he must flush a red color and assure us that the last thing he wanted was for us to leave.

He had hoped that the thirty dollars a day he was being paid would all be profit. He acknowledged our presence and our demands to the extent of giving Sally another two dollars a day for her marketing.

● ● ●

As boarders we were quickly privy to the inner work-ings of the Culpe household. We were the first persons ever to be given the benefit of being, as Quin Culpe told us, smiling, just prior to one of his ongoing attempts to deprive us of food or furniture or the use of the living room, "a part of the family."
We didn't want it, this "benefit."
It wasn't the description in any case but the *reason* for it, our *presence*, that made us know more than we wanted to know.

As we were introduced into the Colony we saw that the general sense held of Quin Culpe was that he was a gal-lant, a devil with the ladies on the dance floor, always up for a good game of tennis; in short, a social asset in this place where people made their own entertainment.

Mavis Culpe was a dry stick who took alarm whenever she was made public, shy to the point of being back-ward.
When she was elsewhere than her own home for tea and was offered a choice of pastries her voice would trail away to nothing as she said, "Oh, I really shouldn't. . . ."
Her gesture, even as she reached for a small cake on the

offered tray, would falter as if she meant to draw back. Her hostess would wait, knowing Mavis to be a hesitator, and a cake would be chosen, would be grasped, and would waver its way into Mavis Culpe's limbo.

She might have been different without Quin to recite a nightly litany of her public shortcomings.
"Then you . . . " we would hear his voice in the darkened house.
"And then you . . .", his bookkeeper's mind clicking and tabulating.
His voice came down through the ceiling into our bedroom.
He went on and on.

Quin Culpe encouraged his daughter to despise her mother as he did.
There was a nightly drama of Virginia's bedtime.
"It's your bedtime, darling," Mavis would be pleading from the start.
Virginia would look at her father.
He would read his paper.
He would pay no attention.

"Go upstairs, dear, and put on your nighty."
Virginia's father would not look up until she rose grudgingly to her feet and began to make her way to the stairs.
"Well, sweetheart, I haven't given you any time today. Come over and sit on my lap."
"Oh, Quin," Mavis would say.

The daughter, Virginia, was large for her age and overhealthy, like a child movie-star. She hovered, with her large head and sausage curls, at the edge of her personal lighted stage. At any moment the music might begin. Larger than Shirley Temple in her heyday and without

the range of Hollywood, she was reduced to such
second-rate ploys as standing in the middle of the room
when her mother had ladies visiting, batting her
eyelashes, and saying in ringing baby tones, "Oh! I made
a mistook!"

Her mother would say tiredly, "There, dear, do go and
play."

She was larger than her father, the healthy, hefty child
sitting on his thin legs. She was larger than her father,
larger than her mother, larger than the house, triumphant.

And her father was a sharp-faced little animal peering
around a corner of her, his teeth bared in a grin. The
two of them looked at Mavis, who stood with a smile
catching and losing the outside corners of her mouth.

The hotel was to be built on reclaimed land.

The land could not hold the weight of the proposed building.

The weight of the building would cause it to slowly sink into the ground.

Axel and the chief engineer walked over the site, blueprints in hand.

This was the land and here was the first problem.

"Doesn't register a thing!" Mavis whispered in my ear. "Not a thing!"

She moved nearer the platform where the old man sat behind a desk, his eyes overlooking his store, where everything necessary to civilized life could be found. She trilled, "Hello, Mr. MacDougal!"

He looked down at us. I don't think he recognized Mavis but that must have been a common experience for him. When the world caught his attention it knew him, who he was, where he was. He smiled.

He was angelic, the innocence of his smile.

"And there's Gordon!"

Mavis loved having me in tow. She would introduce me to someone with a nervous flurry, a busyness.

Gordon was young and sturdy. He wore a blue shirt with a white collar. He longed for Paris and London. He sat on the platform beside his father and drew line drawings of Marlene Dietrich.

He was my dear friend.

He said to me about Zaydie, when she didn't accept an invitation to come sailing, "She thinks you mean to push her overboard!"

Of course she wouldn't come.

Not even to pull the wool over Alicia's eyes.

When Axel met Zaydie one reason she kept him at arm's
length, or so he told me, was because she was already
having an affair with Alicia's husband, Pawli.
Pawli was head surgeon at the hospital where Zaydie
was a nurse.
It was the only hospital and therefore it was the hospital
where I had gone to have my daughter.
Axel met Zaydie during his visits to me there.
I met Alicia when I took a length of gray silk crepe to
my dressmaker to be made into the dress and hat I
would wear at Government House at the garden party
for the Queen's birthday.
By that time Alicia had heard about Axel from Pawli.
Pawli had told his wife at length about the architect who
was romancing his nurse.
Alicia and I immediately liked each other.
She did what she could to protect me from Axel's
womanizing; that is she never mentioned it except to
imply that he only flirted.
And I protected her the same way.
I didn't ever tell her that she was hearing so much from
her husband because he was covering his own traces.
I had my own idea of how it was and I adhered to it.
Elsa Lanchester and I just loved it when Axel had a nice
little flirtation going.
It made him so cheerful.

Alicia knew more about me than I did.
I felt it more than I could acknowledge. It would have
taken a whole new theory for that shift.
At the least pang I would retreat to that prepared place.

I wouldn't have pushed Zaydie overboard.
I would have been enclosed in my own little functioning
idea.

The bed had an iron frame painted white with footrails rising high enough to hold a small metal box on hooks. In that white box, swaddled in soft blankets, was my daughter.

If she fussed I could stretch my leg and rock her iron cradle with my toe.

My stomach was cramping, stitches in my tender parts were made of catgut and rapidly drying to needles but I felt fine.

I was ahead of the schedule, precocious; only twenty and already a completed item.

Here's myself, set to go dancing, there's the infant, there comes the husband bringing flowers.

One of the things the mind does is give us in our head what we'll never have in our hands.

If the line of thought is high-minded we think we're idealistic. If it's wanting a million dollars it's only what would be ideal. In either case the real gets trashed, or at least bruised.

At the most wonderful moment someone can say, "Now this would really be perfect if only . . ." and the projection slides into place adjacent to what only a moment before was as good as it could be.

What passes for idealism is often nothing more than a lousy mental habit.

And sometimes what passes for idealism is more like: it-takes-all-the-encouragement-we-can-imagine-just-to-face-the-day.

Usually it's an almighty mix and medley of all of the above plus more.

When Axel showed up as my loophole in a tattered condition I didn't see myself as ruined and on the run. I saw myself as an artist enroute. Things like Axel happen to people like artists, who lead full and interesting lives.

There was something akin to idealism in my belief that I

deserved it, however unlikely.
I left home so my presumptions could be aspirations.

I never recovered from the social change and the leg up
that marriage gave me.
When I think that marrying Axel displaced me I have to
remember just how displaced I was when we met.
I was capable of being married by an FBI agent and
thinking I knew what was going on.

Lying in my "private room," a partitioned-off bit at the
end of the barracks room that was the hospital's mater-
nity ward, rocking my daughter's cradle, a sea breeze
through the window, the future I perpetually day-
dreamed had shrunk to the immediate and the possible.

• • •

The baby was asleep in the house and Axel and I sat on
the seawall.
The blue sky tended to mauve with the sunset, became a
darker pink shot with orange, became a pinked purple as
oncoming night shifted the balance. Through it all the
still water reflected the changes, merging with the
horizon to make it disappear. The sky passed overhead,
curved and returned to lap at the wall where we sat.
Boats and mooring posts were strokes of black and
floated in mid-air. A pelican threw itself in a downward
fall, head first, into the darkening mauve of the water,
somersaulted and bobbed there, its long beak pointed to
heaven while it swallowed.

There was, briefly, before the advent of Zaydie, a period
of fruition, an enjoyment and sense of well-being that
bordered on delight. A blissful state that love, given all
the modern domestic ramifications, might be.

Quin came from the kitchen holding a plate in each hand.

"Welsh Rarebit!" he announced and returned to the kitchen for more plates.

The plates held a single piece of fried bread with cheese melted over the top.

Quin's tone of voice as he extolled the delights of Welsh Rarebit was the voice adults use with chldren to make a murky fact seem joyous and acceptable.

"Lovely carrots!" Mothers say to con their infants.

Very well then, Welsh Rarebit.

Three of the adults at the table ate heartily. Without fanfare we finished our piece of bread and cheese in about six bites, only to see that Quin was making a project of his. He manipulated his cutlery as if he were about a more complex business. He took minute bites and savored each bite.

When he saw us sitting as if we waited, which we were doing, he said, "The cook is washing up."

"I can get more for myself. She needn't be bothered," and I stood with my plate in hand.

"Oh no!" Quin's mind flashed panic. He had gone to great lengths to convince the Raasloffs that Sally would not tolerate anyone in her kitchen. He meant to keep them on strict rations if he could manage it. No casual evening snacking.

"I *can* ask her to make more," he said.

His face was hurt with the unfairness of it. He was outraged by the greed but in all decency must conceal it. His face twitched.

No one had realized there was no more.

Now it was obvious.

It was meant to be a coup.

"Yes, thank you," Axel said. "We would like more. And perhaps some fruit."

I still stood holding my empty plate.

Dickens in the tropics.

"Would anyone else care for more?" Quin castigated himself.

Mavis insisted that she was quite content, thank you.

"That was quite enough for me. Quite enough," she babbled.

Quin's glare, which seemed to say that hanging would have been good enough for her, shut her up. He left off glaring before she could misunderstand and think he wanted her to want more.

I once heard Quin describing the room he rented to us. We were all out to dinner, which happened, fortunately, often.

He made our bedroom sound as if it were an excursion tour to exotic places. Directly on the water with fishing boats and the sunset laid on. He stopped short at nightly dancing in the ballroom.

"He wasn't always like this," Mavis told me one morning. She hated it that Quin so exposed himself at home and we were there to see it. She would rather be thought dull than pathetic.

Quin Culpe had received a letter in the morning mail. He sat holding it and went into a kind of trance.

He sat and continued reading one page of the letter. Time passed.

An hour passed and he sat reading his page.

In fact he was not reading. After this first time I often saw him caught in this same catatonia.

Mavis came into the bedroom where I was and wept.

"He was the most gentle man I ever knew. But they took him prisoner and when he came home he was like he is now."

It was worse than she could say. Faded and desperate, she was weighed down to the insignificance of a third-rate charwoman by her self-centered undersize husband and her vivacious oversize daughter. Her voice was a whining whisper. Her highest hope was to be overlooked. It was made more bearable by an explanation. She was not a victim of her husband. She was, with so many others, a victim of the war.

Perhaps, equally possible, he *had* been gentle, caught in that brief flare of romance, the wartime honeymoon the couple had had.
Then, returned after the war, he became himself again.
The honeymoon is over.
Returned home, did his altered being content him?
Was it as satisfying for him to make his wife miserable as it had been to make her happy?

Was it, simply, the same?
An equation of the emotions: X is to Y as A is to B.

• • •

Quin Culpe didn't matter as much as these pages have made him seem.
The memories I have of him are bombastic and demanding, as he was.
It's often the case that bombast wins.
The rest of us desperately invent Democracy and fairplay and such like overviews to slow the despots down.

There was one last incident from that time in that house.

I heard Mavis cry out in pain and came out of my bedroom to find her doubled over, holding the bulk of her
belly in both arms.
On the stairs above her Virginia stood, triumphant.
She looked at me, the unexpected observer, with a
hatred totally unchildlike. Her curls and face combined
to make a Medusa mask.
"I tripped on the stairs," Mavis gasped to me, her face
white.
"I fell against the . . .", and she looked around for
something hard to have fallen against.
"Sit down. Let me get you some tea," and I helped her to
the couch, tucked an afghan around her.
All three of us knew that Virginia had kicked her.

"You're not supposed to go in the kitchen!" Virginia spat
while I put water to boil and took down a brown earth-
enware teapot.
"That's the teapot for *Sally!*" the child glared. "*I'm* not
going to drink any tea made in *that* pot!"

When the tea had brewed I poured milk in a cup,
poured tea, added sugar, gave it to Mavis.

• • •

For three months, of necessity, we shared that house.
We would have been there another three months if
Axel had not seen our own house through its building.
When he visited it and saw how far behind it was, saw
the quality of the help, he insisted; and Mr. Sinclair,
who was perhaps not all that unknowledgeable concern-
ing the Culpes, agreed that it needed to be pushed along.

In any case the hotel was being drastically delayed by
the newest plan to drive reinforced concrete pilings into

the reclaimed land as a solution to its instability. The rods that were to be the reinforcement must be shipped from England.

So Axel did have the time.

The house was finished and we moved into it.

Just that half mile was enough to shrink Quin Culpe to lifesize and Mavis to a distant domestic tragedy.

The club.
Government House.
The American Consulate.
The market.
The airport.
The length of Queen Street.
All the private houses.

All in the same land locked showboat.

All the plots, however small, had a beginning, middle, and end.
As the American couple who hired Ethel Golong for a cook.
She was a witch but they were too intelligent to believe in such things. Thin and bent with a bandanna tied hard around her head and an evil glare, she shuffled and muttered spells as she worked around in their house. Which they ignored, not wanting to embarrass her.
To eat a meal at their house — the food was unbelievably bad — was to come under Ethel Golong's evil eye.
They fired her at last and she laid down an obeah so powerful that no one in the colony would work for them.

For some time the blond pants-suited wife was at the market by six to do her day's shopping. She did her laundry by hand.
They began to find little bags of bones and rubbish on the doorstep. When the bags moved into the house and under the pillows on their bed they appealed to the police.

It was as good as a public holiday, I heard, the day two sturdy young policemen, immaculate in starched khaki, dragged the old woman to the house and with an au-

dience of silent spectators, her eyes walling in all directions, she removed the obeah.

• • •

On the second-floor veranda of the house across the
street the two Delara girls and their mother had begun
their day of slow rocking in the shade. Each was
equipped with a rocking chair, a fan, and a glass of iced
fruit juice.

The hotel manager, who was prematurely hired by the
CDC and now had at the least two years of time on his
hands, with salary, had begun to court the elder of the
Delara girls.

The two girls had been kept drastically intact their
whole lives against just such a possibility.

The manager was given a plan of behavior that must be
adhered to.
His conduct was one side of a transaction. The other
side was this young woman's guaranteed condition. She
was untouched. She had never even been to a dance.
She had never walked on the street without the company of her mother or her father.

The suitor found himself dancing a very courtly dance
indeed.
He had to make a daily call in the cool of the afternoon
and sit on the veranda with his beloved and her sister
and her mother.
When the father came onto the porch the suitor would
rise, shake hands all around and leave.
Two times a week he was invited to stay to dinner.
He brought flowers daily and candy for the mother on
the days he stayed to dinner.

He sometimes sailed with us and we asked him every question we could think of apropos his wooing. Between Axel and myself we asked everything.
He answered every question as well as he could. He had no compunction, no feeling of sacred privacy. That delicacy must have been used up in the actuality.

He was fascinated.
He had never in his life met a virgin with a guarantee.
The eroticism inherent in that daily prospectus was more than he had ever known.
It seemed that the two years he had would be just about what he needed to bring so intricate a courtship to its happy resolution.

• • •

I put on dark glasses, took up my basket, went down the stairs to pass underneath the house. It was cool there and dark, with the slight sharp sound of mosquitos.
I said good-morning to Rosa where she washed clothes. She came daily to wash what had been dirtied since the day before and iron what she had washed the day before.

I walked onto the bright street.
The sky was as high as the sun.
Through all that distance the heat fell to ripple on the cement sidewalk.
The Delaras looked down, watched me along the street.
The street was their daily theater.
I wondered whether, in their scheme of things, it was indecent even for a married woman to walk out alone.
Probably it was.

"Must be quite a change for you, eh, Mrs. Raasloff, this weather?"

"Oh, it's very hot and dry where I come from, Sir John."
Sir John continued on past yard goods where I was
choosing enough gray silk crepe for a dress and to cover
a hat.
"Morning, Mr. MacDougal! Morning, Gordon!"
He gives them the same slight salute he has given me.

Mr. MacDougal gives Sir John's unseeing back the same
nod and sweet smile he dispenses to all who pass. He is
unable to distinguish between his customers and his em-
ployees and his old friends.
Monday through Friday he is "at work."
He sits, mildly gazing from his chair, on the platform
that lets him overlook the store.
He is becoming transparent. The color is fading from his
skin and his hair. His eyes are a blue so pale it's as if the
sky shows through his head.
He is driven to the store every morning by a chauffeur.
He is driven home at midday.

Gordon always walked.

Mr. MacDougal didn't want to stay home afternoons
but his strength failed him.

He didn't come to work one morning because he had
died the night before.

Gordon's mother, Ivy, needed Gordon at home evenings.
She could bear his going to the store in the daytime but
he must be home at night.
And Gordon also began to fade.

Of course he was saddened by his father's death; but he
was devastated by his mother's demands.

Now that Mr. MacDougal was not there to spoil the projection, she meant that she and Gordon would share a delightful household forever.

She expected to be invited wherever Gordon was invited as if she were his wife. Often it was not appropriate or the hosts didn't realize she felt as she did and Gordon would be invited on his own.

Many times he didn't go. He went only when it mattered to him so much that he would face his mother's reproach.

I would visit him at the store and we would plot ways to get him out of the house so his mother would be left feeling the least breach of trust.

I am not talking about the time immediately after his father's death.

I am talking about months later.

Ivy realized that our house was where Gordon might often end up, whatever his righteous errand had been. She suspected he came to our house and enjoyed himself.

She would telephone us and ask to speak to him. Sometimes he was with us and sometimes he wasn't. Since she waited up for him the calls could come as late as two in the morning.

The telephone would ring in the dark living room.

The baby would wake and begin to cry.

One of us would fight our way through the mosquito net that surrounded our bed at night and make our way to the telephone, knowing it would be Ivy MacDougal. There was no hope that she would hang up first if we let the telephone ring.

It was a way she punished us for giving Gordon another place to be than home.

A long afternoon.
All the time in the world.
The flowering lane opens out and we have been brought to the heart of the camp. Barracks buildings spread out over an expanse of flat ground. They are beautified by plantings of croton and bougainvillaea and the perpetual orange-red hibiscus.
Inside one of the buildings voices rise and fall.

". . . just when the cook brought it in she dropped it. A whole turkey! It simply slithered off the platter and bounced along the floor. We were stunned! I had *no* idea of what to do. The *Governor! And* Sir John and Lady Agatha. I had *nothing* else I could feed them! *Then* the cook said, "Should I take this turkey back to the kitchen, Ma'am, and bring the *other* turkey in?""

". . . this beastly crowd . . ."

"How *does* one avoid hearing the story of the 1930 hurricane from Mr. Frazier?"
"One avoids Mr. Frazier."

A long afternoon into a long evening. Dinner and dancing.
Does it sound trivial?
A useless and airy waste?
It was more than vanity and a lack of purpose that made me love it.
I was in the right place in the nick of time.

• • •

What mattered was the entirety.
For the first time in my life I felt secure and acceptable, the faults covered over. I believed it too, that I had ar-

rived at my "true" person, I was sweet-natured, young, a good dancer; I was someone I could live with.
Being with Axel had given me this, and my suffusion of contentment was love, in my imagination.
I never trembled because I'd see him in the next moment. But marriage precludes that tremble in any event, doesn't it? Even for the most impassioned, doesn't constant proximity do that tremble in?
"But I wanted *more!* I wanted *more!*" is wailing in my head back of this rationale.

It was all much as Axel had proposed it would be.
And I was apparently all he had hoped.

But what mattered was the entirety.
For the first time in my life the vocabulary I had got from books and the vocabulary I used in conversation meshed.
That's not trivial.
And I saw a variety of women, all unique and, with Mavis the exception, articulate. They all, with Mavis the exception, led forthright lives.
And all the stories were overt.
That *does* reduce the isolation.

• • •

At the far end of the room the Sergeant-Major is singing.
"*Ahnd it's awlroit in the summertoim . . . In the summertoim it's LOVERLY . . . Whoil me old man's paintin 'ard . . . Oim posin in the old back yard . . .*"
The Sergeant-Major is feeling no pain and is a hit.
"Isn't it a silly shame that Sergeant-Majors aren't issued a decent dress uniform?" Richard, the dark-haired subaltern asks.

"I didn't know they weren't."

"They have to wear *that!*"

The Sergeant-Major is wearing freshly washed, starched and pressed khaki, a tunic, and tropical issue shorts. He seems untouched by any sense of being among the peacocks though it is true that the commissioned officers all wear black dress trousers with a satin stripe down the side, a white dress shirt, white mess jacket and red cummerbund, and are very dashing.

"Babies, wet behind the ears," Richard says, "nineteen and twenty years old. They're given a commission because of the school they've gone to and they're sent out to order troops about. Well, *that's* the man that keeps them from making bloody fools of themselves. He makes them look good in front of the men, makes them look like officers!"

The Sergeant-Major's wife is smiling, large-bodied, comfortable.

She likes it that he has this turn in him.

She is as quiet as the chair she sits in but comes alive to beam when the catch phrases of her husband's songs draw a laugh.

She wears a blouse of pink satin with masses of carefully ironed ruffles settled over her broad bosom, and a brown tweed skirt.

"But it's oh! oh! in the wintertoim . . . It's anuvver fing, you know . . . Wiv a little red nose . . . Ahnd very little clothes . . . Ahnd the stormy winds do blow-oh-oh . . . Ahnd the stormy winds do blow!"

"They didn't give hurricanes names in those days! They hadn't had a hurricane in living memory. Nobody knew what was happening. When the eye came people went back outdoors. Then it hit again. Well, she was pulling

at her two pickneys, two little girls, to get them into the
old government building. That's the post office now.
That piece of tin roof came sailing on the wind, took her
head off clean as a knife. Abner ran out and pulled in the
babes just ahead of the tidal wave."

"Old Jenk rode his boat right through the main streets of
this town on that tidal wave. When the water dropped
he had to have his boat dragged to the river. Then he
went down the river to the ocean."

Mr. Frazier is in his sixties. His skin is pink and white.
His hair is white. He wears a white suit. Every evening
at sunset he walks his two white, fluffy dogs on the
foreshore.
"When they were clearing the mud away they found her
body but they never found her head."

The regiments stationed here and in Jamaica tradition-
ally go on to actual fighting, if there is actual fighting to
go on to. For some time now, there always is.
The Gloucestershires went from here to Korea, where a
battalion was massacred down to forty survivors.

• • •

Do you believe that we must "deal" with the past?
Remember it, however imperfectly, sift through the
bits, have it in mind again, this time as if one *knows*
something?
Psychiatrists say so but they're so greedy for prov-
enance. They want everything. To be our all in all.
Then the hour's up and we walk outside into the
weather, get into a car, head for the freeway.

You're blessed if you've never been on the road and driving, semi-mindless, and from nowhere been struck to the heart by remorse.

It's a thing the mind does.

In the almighty list of things the mind does, remembering looms large. As immediate as reaching for the cup you just put down.

The subheadings are a list longer than your arm.

The remembering mind fills in the gaps.

In French class when I was asked to translate and I hadn't studied the lesson my mind would leap at meaning in anything I thought I recognized.

"Since I gave those fools my city they've been fools there."

Mademoiselle would look at me, a blank look of dislike.

"Sometimes the city lifts its roof and looks out just to see what kind of day it is."

"Sit down, please," Mademoiselle would say coldly and go on to someone she could count on.

In Belize, young and ignorant as I was I have no idea of how often my foolishness was covered over by social manners, no one to say "Sit down."

("You only horrified me once, my dear," Alicia said years later in London. "It was when you came to play tennis and you were wearing black shorts and a red shirt!")

The remembering mind justifies after the fact.

"I don't understand why every time you talk about that marriage you deprecate yourself for having been there. It was a very real piece of luck and you took it. It was obviously a godsend. Why do you think you did something wrong?"

"I really do believe that the only reason to marry some-body is because you love them."
And Dr. Baum laughed, probably to show me it was laughable.

The remembering mind keeps it real, recognizes error, regains perspective given the new context.
You know that chill when you've identified something at a distance by sight or sound and it's come nearer to be something equally understandable but it's something else?
There's a chill, a split second, while the mind makes the shift.
Then it's, I used to be wrong but now I'm right.

I used to think I wanted to be a sophisticate, but now I see it's not in me.
I'll forever be just me again pushing hope and theory in lieu of experience, and backing it up with a little bit of courage and a lot of ignorance. (My grandmother said, "You don't have to be ashamed of having ignorance and lice. You just have to be ashamed of keeping them.")

When Axel got Zaydie (and then others) to bed, it was shattering to me. I hadn't expected to be shattered, not according to the theory of the able sophisticate who is one because she says so.
Axel didn't notice I was feeling it, that he was jubilant at his run of luck.
After all he was only being consistent.

The remembering mind creates a future by remember-ing that there is one because there always has been. Like a watch that won't work reminds you of time.
I recovered and got on with my own living.
Hope's a floater but a little esprit-de-gumption is as good

as credit.
And there was even a relief in it, that love wasn't there
and wouldn't be.
Nothing was really changed.

Of course it would have been better to have had that
marriage be a permanent possibility with "daisies pied
and violets blue"; to have been in love and loved back.
But Axel and I didn't join that statistic.
And once it was clear to me that the way we were was
the way we would be, and the six months of grieving for
that fact was past (down really deep I was the only one
who knew it), then it became not all that much a lost
love: more like a theory that fell short.

• • •

The Sergeant-Major has begun to sing, *"If you peek in my
gab-zee-bo when you are passing by . . ."*

Joan has had two ducks stolen.
"You *know*, my dear, I'd *never* have eaten them. But
somebody has *stolen* them and *eaten* them. It makes me
furious to think that someone has had the *good* of my
two ducks!"

*"You'll see a sight that will dee-light the most fabs-tid-ee-us
eye!"*

Joan's daughter, who is eighteen, has begun to flirt with
sweet-faced Richard who is nineteen and, by his own
admission, wet behind the ears.

If the Sergeant-Major were singing Brecht he could ask,
"Ah, where will we all be a year from today."

Sometimes I feel I live in this world like a tenant.
If I didn't see that a lot of people feel the same I'd think it
came from being born a Texas Baptist.

"Just passing through" is a religious term where I came
from.

All the Baptists were stopping just long enough to pick
up their tickets. Their lives were a perpetual middle and
their destinations straight up or straight down.

This "middle" worked them from light to dark, "from
can to can't," all the week long with the weather for
them or against them.

Back-breaking just begins to describe it. It was face-
breaking, hope-breaking. (One year when it looked like
my Uncle Peter was going to make a crop after having
had to plant three times [the first time a dust storm got
it, the second time a heavy rain packed the seed down]
then he fell into his harrow and messed up his leg so that
it took three operations and every penny he had to set it
straight.)

Then on Sundays they'd dress in their best and stand in
some old board building and sing, *"Oh, this is like heaven
to me . . . This is like heaven to me . . . I've crossed over Jordan
to Canaan's fair land . . . And this is like heaven to me."*
If you think that sounds desirable you weren't there.
And you probably grew up in the city.
I remember it as how to live with heartbreak.

When I got my body back from the Baptists I resisted
religion with rules thereafter. Like an allergy.

"You don't believe in heaven, do you?" Alicia asked, her
voice sad. She knew the answer.
She wasn't going so far as to ask whether I believed in
God; it would have been too devastating.
"No, I don't."
She sighed.

If you don't believe in heaven and hell then you don't
get the simplified up and down.

The pattern is instantly random and the options are
more like something hit the floor and splattered.

It's when you face your own choices that you join the
human "fall."

You come into existence as your own self and there goes
Eden.

And if you decide to not turn into your Mom and Dad,
then whatever your age and however fatuous you are,
what comes next are choices.

For choices you need to have some grasp of the terms.
And the terms won't stand still and let you.

Did you ever go after a cow that didn't want to be
caught?

It walks along in an early morning meadow that's slushy
from the weather and you don't even want to be up that
early but that damned cow has to be milked and you
take the rope to slip it over her head and get on a warm
jacket and mud boots if you're lucky and hit the field.
That cow if it glances around at all doesn't seem to notice you all that much. All it's doing is strolling. And it
strolls just as fast as you walk from the time you've
reached its flank. If you walk faster it strolls faster. If you
run it gives a little spurt and gets well ahead and slows to
a stop then starts strolling again.

The terms stay just that far out in front.

And if you get the rope over and do that morning's milking you haven't gained an inch on this evening's milking
or tomorrow morning's.

"You believe in heaven," I said to Alicia.

"Oh, yes."

"What do you think heaven is like? Do you think you
keep your own body there? Do you keep on being you?"

"Of course I will still be me!

When I was very young I thought heaven must be an
endless meadow where I could ride my horse. In Po-
land, in my family, we were taught to ride very young. I
was much younger than my brothers and sisters so they
all rode very well when it was that I must learn. It
seemed to me that I was the only one in the world who
did not know how to ride a horse. And I was frightened
of horses. I was terrified. Every day I would be crying
when the riding master would put me onto my horse.
My older sister, Heloise, would laugh.

She said I cried so much because I was a gypsy. She was
terrible to me sometimes when we were children. I was
the only one of the children in my family to be dark like
my father's people. Heloise said that my hair was brown
because I was a gypsy. She said the gypsies had left me
on the doorstep and *her* mother and father had taken me
in, but I was not their child.

She said ladies and gentlemen do not cry.

And every time I fell off my horse the riding master
would put me back on again. He was not sympathetic
but he was not cruel. He knew I would learn to ride. He
knew that it was nothing to fall off a horse but it was
everything to stay off.

Then my mother made Heloise stop saying I was a
gypsy, and she told me it was not true.

About that time I learned to stay on the horse.

Then it was the case that I had a talent for riding.

I became the best rider of all my family.

I competed in dressage and jumping and I won many
trophies and ribbons.

It made Heloise heartsick that I was so good.

And I loved it.

So, when I was a child I thought heaven would be an
endless meadow with no fences where I could ride in
any direction and not be stopped."

"When you think of heaven now how do you think of it?"

"I think in heaven we have everything we ever wanted."

We were sitting on the sea wall watching the sunset colors change, feeling the soft freshness of the breeze off the water.

"Alicia," I said, to alleviate her sadness at my fatal declaration, "I *like* living my life. This is like heaven to me."

coda

I've been thinking today, planning a curry, of the sad little wife of the Major, ex-Indian-Army.
She did not cut her wrists when a very usual sexy female arrived to apply for an American visa and on that visit devoured the little Major as if he were a dressed-out partridge. She did cut her wrists on the lady's *second* visit, when the visa was ready and the woman this time around chose to bed with the fat-assed U.S. Vice-Consul. It was having her husband returned to her as rejected goods that undid the Major's wife.

In her happier or at least more felicitous days she taught me to make curry. The last time I saw her (we were to leave the following week) was at an official dance. The Major and his wife were in the Governor's party, which meant they must stand at attention just inside the door while the band, to announce the Governor's arrival, played 'God Save the Queen."
That arrival, her wrists taped so neatly it was decorative, and herself with her eyes straight ahead of her, herself

standing on parade before a roomful of people, most of whom knew her pathetic story to some degree or another.

They were such dowds.
They could never have anticipated such a *romance* as that. (Perhaps that was exactly what won the lady for the Major. Some people of both sexes like nothing so much as to bestow themselves all gift-wrapped to the most unlikely candidate. And then when they choose, to take it all back again.) The Major short and balding, his wife only one more of those incredibly dressed women once to be found in the multitudes living their lives out in backwater British colonies.

The malice of that woman's choice, the dowdy Major, and the ridiculous pathos of the later-known stories, that the wife had bedded down on the couch to save them all from gossip.

I went home from that dance alone, Axel having many young women to say his goodbyes to.
At the club Saturday nights I could say, "Do you know who the most beautiful woman in the room is?" after having watched him ogle the lot.
"That one?"
"No, that one over there in the far corner. In the white dress."
And he would look, as if hypnotized, to agree that yes she was the most beautiful woman in the room and move to join her company.
I was never a contender.

A letter from Gordon says, "How long ago it seems and I have no nostalgia left for those Belize days. Belize too broken and after Hurricane Hattie it was awful. We were not sorry to get away."

And he says, "Where you lived stood. Lindstrom's house was totally down and Sir John was laconic and Lady Agatha mental, I thought, and quite funny and pathetic."

And he says, "Belize, a monumental ruin."

I loved that place and it sometimes seems as if the only friends in my life were there, perhaps forever true, coming as I have to be so ambivalent that I must weigh every piece of cheese pro and con.

Still, if I exaggerate, the place and the people have been changed.

No one left to contradict or distinguish between the memories I stored even as they happened, knowing I would want them later; the sadness in that forethought; I loved it there; a kind of homesickness as if I walked backwards.

And the memories of *now*, rising up, that I didn't know I had.

As when I touched the Major's wife's wrists to say, "Did you hurt yourself?" she winced so deeply I was struck silent.

Remembering only then the bit of story I'd heard that afternoon, why her wrists were bandaged. Wondering, shocked, how I could have forgotten.

How could I have forgotten?

Acknowledgements:

I would like to thank the National Endowment for the Arts and the Briarcombe Foundation/Bolinas for financial assistance during the time I was working on this book.

B.L.H.